" to make love to me,"

Danzer whispered against her cheek. "*Ask* me to make love to you. Say it, Laney. Say it!"

But she couldn't get the words out. They were staggering, enormous words, and as badly as she wanted to, she couldn't get them out. She caught her breath and held it. He understood. Only too well, he understood. "I'm sorry," she whispered.

"We're both sorry," he said. "We both want it to happen, but neither of us is willing to take responsibility for it. A very adult pair, we are."

"I'm sorry," she whispered again.

"Don't beat yourself up, baby. It's not worth it. Believe me, I know."

She couldn't quite meet his eyes. "I guess you've known lots of women, haven't you?" she asked timidly.

He said nothing for a long while, then lifted his hand to her face and tilted her chin back, forcing her gaze up. "Not so many," he said. "And none like you. Not one."

Dear Reader,

Welcome to Silhouette—experience the magic of the wonderful world where two people fall in love. Meet heroines that will make you cheer for their happiness, and heroes (be they the boy next door or a handsome, mysterious stranger) that will win your heart. Silhouette Romance reflects the magic of love—sweeping you away with books that will make you laugh and cry, heartwarming, poignant stories that will move you time and time again.

In the coming months we're publishing romances by many of your all-time favorites, such as Diana Palmer, Brittany Young, Sondra Stanford and Annette Broadrick. Your response to these authors and our other Silhouette Romance authors has served as a touchstone for us, and we're pleased to bring you more books with Silhouette's distinctive medley of charm, wit and—above all—*romance*.

I hope you enjoy this book and the many stories to come. Experience the magic!

Sincerely,

Tara Hughes
Senior Editor
Silhouette Books

ARLENE JAMES

Dream of a Lifetime

Silhouette *Romance*

Published by Silhouette Books New York

America's Publisher of Contemporary Romance

SILHOUETTE BOOKS
300 E. 42nd St., New York, N.Y. 10017

Copyright © 1989 by Arlene James

ISBN: 0-373-08661-X

First Silhouette Books printing July 1989

Printed in the U.S.A.

ARLENE JAMES

grew up in Oklahoma and has lived all over the South. In 1976 she married "the most romantic man in the world," and since then "every trip with him has been a romance to remember forever." We think you will feel the same way about her books.

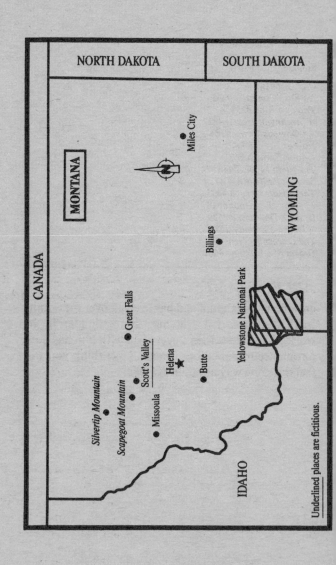

CANADA

NORTH DAKOTA

SOUTH DAKOTA

MONTANA

Miles City

Billings

Great Falls

Silvertip Mountain

Scapegoat Mountain

Scott's Valley

Helena

Butte

Missoula

Yellowstone National Park

WYOMING

IDAHO

Underlined places are fictitious.

Chapter One

The fish arched two feet into the air, its silvery blue body flashing white in the clear morning sun. With a smack it landed on the thick planking of the pier and began flicking its tail in wild, erratic attempts to throw itself back into the water. Gradually the flapping subsided, and the sleek, shining body quivered spasmodically. On her knees, Laney reached for it, careful of the razorlike fins, and the fish arched against her palm with still considerable strength. Using her other hand, she deftly struck it just behind the eye with the blunt end of her knife. Laney winced slightly as the strong tail fluttered a moment longer, then ceased. She tossed it into a slithering pile of a dozen others, each nine or ten inches long.

Already three neatly scaled, sliced and cleaned perch lay in a still row on her father's left. His knife slashed through another, making quick work of the cleaning process. Laney moved to his right and wordlessly took a fish from the pile, scraping it with the notched edge of her knife. For several moments, they worked side by side, kneeling on the wide planks of the dock. Suddenly Hiram Scott's graying head bobbed up, his hands growing still.

Laney stopped and listened, aware of her father's high-tuned senses. He heard something, something she could not pick up. She never ceased to marvel at her father's acute sensitivity. It had always been thus, for Hiram Scott was a man uniquely attuned to his surroundings, as was Laney in her own curious way. The blue, cold, placid lake, the white-peaked mountains, the dark green spikes of the pines and the white-mottled sky were as much parts of Hiram Scott and his daughter as were his hands and her feet. He sheathed his knife and stood.

"The flags," he said. "I forgot to put out the damn flags." Muttering a string of blue, suitably foul words, he knelt at the edge of the pier, leaning far over, and washed his rough hands in the cold, clean water. "The new man, he asked for a signal, damn it, and I said three red flags."

"Well, if he's much of a pilot, he'll know us when he finds us, flags or no flags," his daughter commented idly, going back to her work. "It's not as if he could mistake us for the neighbors, after all."

"He doesn't know the area," Hiram reminded her. "And if you don't know, one valley pretty much looks like another from the air."

"Uh-huh, and the next inhabited valley is forty-five miles from here."

"All the same," he insisted, getting to his feet, "I said three red flags. Don't want him decidin' against us 'cause of somethin' I said I'd do and didn't.''

Laney smiled to herself. If Hi Scott said three red flags, there would be three red flags, for her father's word was his bond. Still, she placed little confidence in any pilot who couldn't find where he was going. What use would he be if he couldn't fly hunting parties in and out of the mountains with the same unerring instinct with which she and her father guided the hunt? She didn't truly understand what was wrong with the old system—a flotilla in summer and a horse pack in winter. She realized that her parents were beginning to feel the strain of three decades of life in the wild Montana Rockies, but they were young yet, and it wasn't as if they had to manage alone.

She had grown up in this valley, playing in the bottom of a canoe, napping to the river's sloshing lullaby, climbing, tracking, exploring, riding. At age eleven she had guided her first group back from Congregation Point with all the confidence and skill of a man twice her age. Of course, two of that first party of four had balked at following a mere child upriver for twenty winding miles. They'd simply climbed back in their truck and headed down the mountain, but the other two had been game, and Laney had encountered only one other party since then who wouldn't get in the river with her.

From that point on, the river had belonged to Laney, except for a few days early each summer that she spent visiting friends and family. In winter, they contracted horse packing from a rancher downriver. She was at home on that river, and she liked the canoe ride down to Congregation, where the Scott family kept a battered old pickup truck. It was as commonplace to her as was a stroll to the corner drugstore to millions of other twenty-three-year-olds the country over, and she frankly didn't care how inconvenient it was to the dozen or so amateur fishermen and explorers she and her parents shepherded each summer through the Rocky Mountain wilderness that was their home.

The past several years, however, the majority of their summer visitors had been children, the offspring of friends and family. While it was more difficult and dangerous to transport children on the river and required her father's help, Laney nevertheless felt a certain loyalty to the old way, and until recently, there had been no other option. Over the years her duties had expanded. Laney now led not only the summer flotilla and several fishing expeditions each summer but many of the fall hunts as well. For some time now the work had been divided pretty evenly between Laney, her mother and her father, and it worked out pretty well. She saw no reason to change it.

Laney finished the fish she was working on and took another, slipping the tip of her knife between two shiny scales, before she heard the distant, droning hum of the airplane engine. Half a minute, she figured. Hi had heard the plane half a minute before she had. Amazing. Quickly she dispatched with the fish and took another, the hum from the sky growing gradually louder. Soon came the distant creak of the pulley as her father hoisted the first of the flags, and then the racket from the plane drowned it out. Suddenly there was a splutter, a mechanical cough, and then instant silence. Curious and slightly alarmed, Laney rocked back on her heels and looked over her shoulder at the sky, one mucky hand shielding her eyes from the sun's crystalline glare. She spotted the small red and white craft immediately, its nose too low and unsteady for a smooth landing, its pontoons wobbling precariously below partially retracted landing gear.

Laney pushed up to her full height, her thick brown hair swaying between her shoulder blades. She held her breath until the engine sputtered alive once more and the plane lifted and banked, circling for another try. Laney shook her head and absently stroked her knife against her thigh, leaving streaks of muck on her jeans. *This guy must be a real winner,* she reckoned with a rueful smile. *Some pilot.* She suddenly felt certain her father would reject him and watched smugly as he revived the engine, circled once more and came in.

It wasn't picture-perfect by any means. The right pontoon dipped slightly more than its twin, and the plane rocked from side to side after its first contact with the surface of the lake. The pilot attempted to right the situation and only managed in skipping. Twice more the plane left the water in tiny, awkward hops, the engine sputtering ominously, before settling rather deeper than seemed desirable and chugging up to the pier.

Laney watched detachedly as a big man with very dark hair eased himself through the small cockpit door. He had a pink nylon rope looped over one shoulder, clashing violently with the tomato-red flannel of his shirt. He wore khaki pants and dark sunshades with gold wire frames and a narrow leather belt cinched around a surprisingly slender waist. The belt, combined with the bright red of his shirt, accented the considerable breadth of his shoulders. He flashed Laney a wide grin and called a deep-voiced hello, then quickly secured the clip at one end of the rope around the strut attaching the pontoon to the fuselage. The other end of the rope he wound around his left hand, as if waiting for permission to tie off.

When he removed his glasses and slipped them into his pocket, she took an instinctive step backward. She wanted nothing to do with this man. This was her father's business, and he would momentarily appear and take the matter in hand. She would have no part of it, and some part of her assumed that this tall, dark-haired man with the broad shoulders and the healthy tan would simply disregard her. It had happened before and often. For some reason it was always the supremely masculine male who failed to see beyond her femininity to the quiet, confident capability that she so treasured, and this, she silently conceded, was a supremely masculine man.

He glanced at the knife held casually in her left hand, and she saw one dark, straight brow arch upward. She glanced over her shoulder, expecting to see her father striding down the pier, only to spy him in the distance, still hoisting that now useless third red flag up the pole standing some hundred yards away. It was up to her then. She turned back, her mouth open to make some appropriate greeting, and did a double take at the big man bearing down on her. Suddenly he was there, brown eyes glistening, white teeth flashing a smile, so close she reeled backward a step, arms akimbo, knife tip turned upward against her body.

"Danzer Wilson," he said, and he reached out for her right hand, encasing it in his own very solid one. Laney's mouth fell open as the slimy muck squished against his palm. She watched the expression on his face change from one of friendly greeting to disgust.

"Ugh!" He yanked his hand back and stared at it. "What on earth?" He backed away, and his gaze fell on the heap of fish beyond Laney's feet. His dark brows came together over the high bridge of a nose that just missed being sharp. "Oh, great!" he exclaimed, stepping quickly to the edge of the pier.

Laney watched as he went down on his haunches and reached toward the water. The plane dipped and bucked as the towline tightened, and still his hand remained some inches above the cleansing water. Reluctantly he stood and glared at her.

"Of all the stupid things to do!"

She lifted her chin, color suffusing her cheeks. "You have some nerve."

"I meant me," he told her dismissively, but her chin stayed high, vibrant light green eyes looking down a small, straight nose at him. He lifted his hand, stared at it, and made a face. "Listen, is there a cloth or a rag of some kind around here?"

Laney looked around her, knowing full well that there wasn't anything of the sort but needing time to think. What would she have done? she wondered. She sometimes dried her hands and face on the tail of her shirt. Unfortunately it was tucked in just now, and as these jeans were a little small, she'd have to unzip them to get it out or lose a button in the process. There had to be something else....

She remembered how she'd cleaned the knife blade earlier. Almost without thought she'd wiped it on the thigh of her jeans. They were years old and so soft they couldn't even hold their shape anymore. If they hadn't been, she couldn't have gotten into them. She wondered why it didn't occur to Danzer Wilson to simply wipe his hand on his pants leg. Then she looked at him. His khakis were new and crisply creased, virtually spotless. Laney set her mouth. Greenhorn. He had it written all over him. It would no more occur to him to wipe his hands on his clothes than to flap his arms and fly.

He was standing there with an oddly expectant expression on his face, his dark eyes watching her with an unnerving intensity, as if she were an exhibit in a zoo and might do something terribly entertaining any moment now. She scowled at him and took a deep, calming breath, reminding herself that this man had been expected, invited. She would be as polite to him as she had been to countless other buffoons over the years, the leering ninnies who brought pistols expecting to bag the great-granddaddy of grizzlies, the boozers who thought they could stroll into the wilderness with a bottle in one hand and a loaded shotgun in the other, the cowards trying to prove there was *something* in life of which they were not afraid, the know-it-alls who spouted their abilities every hour of the day and then got lost going to the latrine. Even isolated as she was from the world at large, she supposed she'd met just about every kind of loon and idiot that existed. She wondered briefly into which category Danzer Wilson would fall. But it hardly mattered. He was standing there with that smelly gunk on his hand and a plane on a rope over his shoulder. Again, it was up to her to do something.

She tightened her grip on the knife, then let it go. It fell with a thud beside her booted foot. Grimly she moved forward, her pale, bright gaze locked on his dark, gleaming one. Standing before him, she realized just how tall he was. She guessed half a foot taller than her, and she stood fully five feet and eight inches in her boots. Still, she felt no intimidation, no fear, no inferiority. Pointedly she wiped her own soiled hand alongside the area where she'd cleaned her knife blade, then fixed him with a steady gaze and turned, bringing her hands to her hips.

The coffee-colored eyes sparkled, and his mouth—a healthy, dusty pink, she noticed, with gently rounded twin peaks in the center of the upper lip and a well-proportioned fullness to the lower—was fashioned in a wide, amused grin, exposing white, even teeth. Only then did she feel a tremor of misgiving, a tensing of muscles, a catch in her breath. Automatically she banished it, conquering this uncertain emotion much as she conquered fear and indecision, by the sheer force of her will.

Her chin came up again, and she gave her head a brave little flip, tossing her long, glossy, golden brown hair off her shoulders. "Do your best," that little gesture said, "I'm up to it," and Danzer Wilson's grin widened.

Deliberately, slowly, he wiped his hand across her thigh, first in one direction, then another, his dark eyes holding hers, laughing, taunting. His hand was large and hot and carried a strength that rocked her like a willow in a gusting wind, heating her flesh beneath the soft denim and at the same time sending a shiver up her spine. She hadn't expected this, hadn't anticipated these hot and cold sensations shooting through her, the taunt behind those gleaming eyes, and now that smoldering, speculative look, as if he were measuring her for something, imagining...

Suddenly she was seeing him in a way she hadn't before: the rather angular planes of his handsome face, square jaw, squarer chin; that well-drawn mouth; the shallow creases that appeared when he smiled; the black lashes rimming the clear white eyes with irises the color of coffee beans; the glossy black hair with a straight part streaking back from the left temple of a high, wide, slightly rounded forehead.

For some reason she was aware of subtleties, like the gentle bob of a not-too-prominent Adam's apple when he swallowed, and the throb of a strong, rapid pulse in the thick veins of his neck. She felt the long, heavy fingers of his hand and the hard, clipped edges of his flat, pinkish nails. His feet were large, his legs long and strong and ridged with muscles, his middle flat and hard, his chest wide and deep, his wrists and ankles knobbed with big, dense bones, his arms corded by muscles, his shoulders broad and level and sheltering. Yes, *sheltering*.

At once she recognized that feeling as one she'd felt before. But where? When? With whom? The names and faces of a half-dozen men flitted through her mind: Roger Bernard, the boy she'd dated the spring of her sixteenth birthday while visiting Uncle Clay in Billings; Uncle Clay himself; Uncle Tuck, Aunt Ivy's husband, whom she'd visited in Cut Bank the summer she was twelve; Marty Walker, who lived over in the Cabinets now, taking pictures of wildlife for international magazines; Parker Stand Tall, the Blackfoot Indian who'd come down that winter to help out while Dad's leg had mended from the fall he'd taken up on Silvertip; and George, who'd hauled Dad down—and Dad, too. Yes. And Crater. Undoubtedly Crater. But this man was different from all of them. Every one of those men was Montana bred and born, elemental men for whom the high peaks and the low, wide-open places meant home and good, hard living. There was another man, though, a man she'd known only a short while. Like him, this man was too polished, too *civilized*. Those others were sure, capable, dependable sorts who gave off a comfortable air of confidence, while this man... This man was handsome, devastatingly so, and he radiated a kind of physical magnetism. This, too, she recognized for having met something like it that week in Seattle. It had unnerved her then. It unnerved her now.

She stepped away from the heated hand, feeling vulnerable and somehow guilty, as if the strength she'd sensed in him had made her a traitor to all those other, worthy men in whom she'd placed her trust. Adding insult to injury, he laughed at her, softly, almost soundlessly; yet angry words rushed into her mouth, forestalled only by those of her father as he hurried toward them.

"You must be Wilson. Found us all right, did you? Forgot my flags. Just been raisin' 'em. You've met my daughter, Laney. Got us a good mess of fish there for our dinner."

He came to a halt and stuck out his right hand, his left arm going naturally around Laney's shoulders. Danzer Wilson looked at the hand he'd just cleaned so thoroughly against Laney's thigh. Grinning still, his eyes on Laney, he accepted Hi Scott's firm, welcoming grip.

"Nice to meet you. Guess you could say I've already met both the daughter and the fish."

Hiram glanced over his shoulder at the mound of fish then at Laney, whose eyes were sending daggers at the newcomer. Her palms rubbing against the sides of her legs told their own story. A smile played around the edges of his mouth, and he tightened his arm about his daughter's shoulders.

"Forgot to clean her hands, did she?" he asked in a voice thick with chuckles. "Well, at least she's not finicky. Fish guts don't bother her a bit, and that's a handy thing when your supper comes from the lake as often as not."

Danzer laughed that silent laugh again, and Laney felt fire surging to her cheeks. She glanced at her father from the corners of her eyes, appalled and hurt to see him so visibly relaxed and friendly. He stepped away from her without even acknowledging the glance, as if completely unaware of her feelings! He helped Danzer tie off the anchor line and stuck his head inside the plane to have a cursory look around the craft he was hiring along with its owner and pilot. The two chatted amiably for a couple of minutes about such things as seating capacity and the cost of fuel and the incredible peaks and valleys over which one must fly.

Laney watched them with growing resentment—the craggy, gray-thatched face of her father and the tanned, classical features of Danzer Wilson with his black, well-groomed hair. They were so very different, these two men. How could they get so chummy so quickly? Seemingly, Hiram accepted this man and the change he represented without question. Couldn't he tell that Danzer Wilson didn't belong here? He was usually so aware—and wary—of people. Yet, she'd sensed an obstinacy about him lately, and it had all started with the idea of the air charter. She didn't understand.

Hi said something about coffee and clapped Danzer on the shoulder, reaching up to do so. It struck Laney as they walked toward her that her father had aged considerably this past year. Next to the big, dark handsomeness of Danzer Wilson, he seemed smaller, grayer, and more fragile than she had realized. His bowlegged gait seemed more awkward and stiffer than usual, while Danzer Wilson was a man in his prime, sure, agile, with long, smooth strides. As they passed her, Danzer turned his head and shot her a smug, provocative look, dark brows lifting upward, lips tightening into that infuriating smile, eyes frank and sparkling. It was a look that said he was staying, that he expected to know her better.

"Miss Scott," he said. "If you need some help with the rest of those fish..."

"Don't bother," she snapped, aware of Hi's disapproving frown and the forced smile which quickly followed it. Then they were well past. She pulled a face at his back, grumbling, "Fancy man. Tenderfoot." She strode forward and went down on her knees, grabbing up the knife with a sweep of her hand. She didn't need his help for anything, a man like that, and neither did her father, if only he'd see. And he would. Surely he would. Otherwise her life was going to change in some fundamental way. She sensed it as she sensed a coming change in the weather and the presence or absence of a special friend.

The hair prickled on the back of her neck, and for a long moment she left her work again to stand and stare about her. It was all the same, the white peaks protruding through the dark blanket of trees, the big blue sky above, the cold blue lake below, and the large, solid house of log and rock and handmade brick with the row of outbuildings in back and the smooth bole of the flagpole in front. It hadn't changed and it shouldn't. What her parents had built here deserved to survive intact. She couldn't help feeling that it was somehow threatened.

Laney carried the string of cleaned fish through the heavy planked door and into her mother's stone-flagged kitchen. For some reason the shutters were closed on the window above the tub sink, and it was dark and cool inside, despite the bread baking in the old cast-iron stove in the corner. Laney never looked at that stove without hearing her mother tell how Hi had trucked it from Great Falls, then built a raft to tow it upriver as a wedding present to his bride. Lil Scott loved that old stove as she loved her rambling, eclectic house. In the beginning, it had been a mere two-room log cabin with a storage cellar, but in the quarter-century of her marriage, it had grown into a kind of private lodge. In addition to the great room, there was a second story containing five small bedrooms, each with a window, a sloping ceiling and a door. They opened onto the narrow landing overlooking the large stone room that served as living room, lobby and dining area when the Scotts had guests. Lil and Hiram still occupied the room off the kitchen, and a kind of community bathroom and hallway had been added off of that, complete with a trio of sinks made of lacquered wood and a pair each of rock-walled shower stalls and private cells with real porcelain toilets. The kitchen, however, remained the hub of the household and Laney's favorite room. Today, however, the presence of Danzer Wilson at her mother's pine table ruined it for her.

He was sitting in one of the four ladder-back chairs Hiram had built to replace the benches he had originally crafted along with the rectangular table. Her mother had given him one of her precious china cups, while she and Hiram crowded around one corner of the table and drank their coffee from cheap plastic. A plate of sliced bread sat before him, and he held in his palm a slice plastered with sweet, pale butter.

"I really shouldn't eat another," he said, lifting the thick slice to his mouth.

"Then don't," Laney replied automatically. Her parents turned aghast eyes at her, and she felt her spirits sink a bit further. Quickly she dumped the fish in the sink.

"Can't resist," Danzer was saying between bites. "If this is a true example of the food around here, I'm going to have to climb that mountain just to stay fit."

"Lillian's more than a fair cook, Dan," Hiram bragged, "even when I don't give her much to cook with."

"You'll have him thinking we go hungry, Hi," his wife scolded affectionately. "Truth is, Mr. Wilson, we always have plenty. There's venison and mutton and fowl in season, and I give up the odd hen now and again. And of course there's the fish, perch, trout and white, and way up there's kokanee and silver salmon. And there's berries to put up and pine nuts for grinding and roasting, and I keep a vegetable patch every summer, so we can have fresh at least one season a year. Then there's the calf. We'll have fresh beef in late winter, and of course Hi and Laney make a supply run every few weeks. Sometimes in deep winter we get more than our fill of canned ham and hash, but all in all I think we've got it better than most city folk.''

"I believe you, Mrs. Scott," Danzer said, "but I'd be pleased if you'd call me by my given name."

"That seems natural enough, and I'm just plain Lil."

"Oh, not plain, surely, not by any standard, but Lil it is and gladly."

Laney almost gagged on the sugary words. Her mother was still a good-looking woman, to be sure, with the same long, brown hair as her daughter and a trim, firm figure. Like Laney, she was tall, and her eyes were the same bright green. With her hair swept up into a curling ponytail and her smooth, honey-colored skin still unlined, she looked more like Laney's older sister than her mother. Still, it galled Laney to hear Danzer Wilson praise her.

Her back to them, she ran a few inches of water into the sink to keep the fish from smelling up the room, and after the din of water falling into the metal tub had ceased, she made a show of drying her hands on Lil's bleached tea towel while turning to face Danzer.

"Suppose you tell us something about yourself," she said, pointedly addressing him. Danzer took another big bite of his bread and chewed it leisurely, his elbows on the table.

"Well, let's see," he said at length. "I'm thirty-five, single, healthy. I'm from Illinois, and I've traveled a bit, but not enough to really see anything of the world, I'm afraid. I don't have much family, one sister, older than me, and two nieces. Guess the girls are fourteen and sixteen now, at that busy age when uncles don't mean much. Then, of course, there's my brother-in-law and a few close friends." His dark eyes seemed to seek out Laney's. "You could say I'm unattached. That's about it."

Not quite, Laney thought, folding her arms. Aloud she said, "And how do you make your living?"

Danzer Wilson turned slightly in his chair, an odd little smile on his lips. "Oh, some of this and some of that," he replied smoothly, his eyes on a knot in the tabletop. "Right now, I'm a pilot." He looked up and smiled broadly at Hi and Lillian. "That is, if I'm hired."

Both the elder Scotts laughed good-naturedly. "Shoot, man, are you sure you want to spend the next three months on this mountain?" Hiram asked. "It can get mighty tedious if you don't like the out-of-doors."

Danzer smiled. "Hi, I'll tell you the honest truth. I've never gotten around to much hunting or fishing, but it's always been a dream of mine to live like this. You've got a very real and immediate kind of freedom here, and—" Laney felt the shock of his gaze on her face, and heat began spreading upward from her shoulders "—I find the scenery positively breathtaking."

She was embarrassed and angry enough to slap him. It wasn't the least bit fair or proper of him to sit coolly and stare at her with her parents right there at his elbow! But when she looked to Hi and Lillian, their attention was fixed blandly on Danzer Wilson, as if Laney herself was not even in the room, as if he was staring out a shuttered window at the pines and the mountain that reared up majestically behind them. She wanted to cry and stomp her feet like a child until they woke from this charm-induced stupor and saw the man for what he was: an outsider who couldn't belong, a mistake. He ought not to be here, he'd admitted it himself.

"It's not much salary," Hi was saying.

Danzer nodded. "Suits my needs, though, and with room and board and the opportunity to do some things I've wanted to do all my life, well, it seems perfect to me."

"It's settled then!" Hiram Scott whacked a fist on the tabletop. "By jig, this is going to work out. We're going to have us a first-class little operation here. I knew it the moment I spoke to that Whatley fellow from the Department of Fish, Wildlife and Parks."

"Carl Whatley's a friend of mine. We went to school together," Danzer said. "When I spoke to him about the kind of situation I wanted, he said he'd put out some feelers. I didn't know until he'd already talked to you that he was putting out those feelers by shortwave radio. You just don't think about those kinds of things when you're used to a telephone in every room of the house."

"Maybe you'd be more comfortable in that house with all those telephones," Laney mused, but Danzer Wilson shook his head.

"I don't think so, not a bit. In fact, I'm ready to settle in right now. It sounded so good I came prepared."

Laney was stunned, but her mother came gracefully to her feet, a welcoming smile on her face.

"That's grand, Danzer. The room isn't made up yet, but that won't take long, and there's plenty of fish for dinner. Laney, you'll get some fresh linens, please, and make up the bed in the north room." She looked at her daughter to be certain she had understood, and wrinkled her nose, adding, "but change your clothes first." She turned back to the men immediately. "Hi, help him get his gear off that plane. Do you play chess, Dan? Hi and Laney will want to take you on. I like cards myself. Ever heard of Penny Gin?"

"That's a new one on me," he admitted, dwarfing them all as he stood. "But I have to warn you up front, I'm a hard man to beat at anything. It's in my nature to play to win."

Braggart, Laney thought, but her father simply clapped him on the shoulder, the corners of his eyes crinkling in merriment.

"We'll have to give him a try then, won't we, Laney?"

"Indeed we will," she answered tersely, and Danzer Wilson grinned, locking eyes with her.

"I look forward to it."

Laney held his gaze, accepting the challenge, though angry and even a little panicked if she had been honest with herself. He seemed to think he could just drop in here out of the sky and have everything his own way, charm people who ought to know better, take on the mountain and all comers, and conquer them all with nothing more than his handsome face and glib words. Well, she knew better. Not everyone was as easily charmed as her parents seemed to be, and the mountain cared nothing for people or their words. A man's actions decided his fate out here, not good looks and not charm. So let him smile. He couldn't charm the mountain, and he couldn't charm her. They wouldn't let him in, either of them. He could stay—but he couldn't belong.

Chapter Two

Laney stood at the foot of the bed and shook out the sheet so hard it cracked like a whip. Danzer laughed as he unzipped the first of two large, navy blue nylon bags.

"I take it making beds is not among your favorite things to do."

"I don't mind," Laney told him, making the first fold on a neat, hospital corner, "usually."

"Ah." He didn't miss her meaning, but it didn't seem to trouble him overmuch, either.

She watched from the corner of her eye as he laid folded articles of clothing on the open, narrow shelves that flanked one side of the door. Between the corner of the wall and the frame of the shelves hung a naked wooden rod. This constituted his "closet." All the other upstairs rooms, except Laney's, contained similar arrangements. Laney's had been torn down to make room for the carved, dark cherry wood bedstead and the large, matching wardrobe that she was given on her twenty-first birthday. Like her mother's stove, the gas generators that powered their electricity, all the mattresses in the house and many of their supplies, both pieces of furniture had been towed upriver on a raft.

Laney finished the sheet and unfolded an ivory-colored down comforter over the bed. Even in July, nights were often cool enough to warrant such cover. Rarely did she find it necessary to kick off the covers at night in order to sleep comfortably, and those unaccustomed to the northern climate usually required more insulation than the natives of the area.

A small bedside table and a chair placed in the far corner were the small room's only other furnishings, both so rough that small sections of bark still clung to their various pieces. A braided rag rug covered the floor between the door and the bed, and a beaver pelt was tacked to one log wall. A candle in a hand-carved wooden holder shaped like a bear and a sachet made of a pine cone stuffed with bits of cinnamon, nutmeg and cloves sat on the table. Overhead hung a single light bulb fitted with a shade made of tanned hide stretched over a wood frame, and along the wall that faced the landing, near the floor, were a series of long, narrow slits that allowed some heat to drift in from the fire kept going day and night in winter in the fireplace of the great room. All in all, it was rather primitive. Laney knew that, but she thought it beautiful in its simplicity and its harmony with their surroundings, and she had awakened in a toasty bed in a frigid room for so long that she didn't even consider it a hardship.

She could not help noticing that Danzer Wilson's clothes looked peculiarly out of place in that small, primitive room. For one thing, everything looked new. The jeans were too blue, the khakis too crisp, the flannel shirts too stiff, the sweaters unpilled. The bright red, down-filled jacket he hung up even had the tags still attached, and the brown suede lace-up boots he placed on the floor beneath it were virtually unmarked. Danzer Wilson was not what he wanted them to believe he was. The clothes, she decided as she pulled a slip over the pillow, like the room, did not fit him somehow. She tossed the pillow onto the bed and turned to leave.

"Thanks," he said, leaving the second bag unpacked on the floor.

"Don't worry about it," she replied stiltedly, "and don't expect it to happen again. From now on you make your own bed. There's no maid service here, you know. This isn't a hotel."

His implacable smile unnerved her, and for some reason it angered her. He hooked his left elbow on the edge of a shelf and cocked his head, smile in place.

"You just can't bring yourself to like me, can you?"

"How can I like someone I don't know?" she replied.

He scratched his ear. "Your parents seem to like me well enough."

"Maybe they're more trusting than I am."

"Never take anything or anyone at face value; is that it?"

She folded her arms and fixed him with a cool stare. "Not really. I find most people are just what they seem to be."

"Then I'm the only one you've formed an instant dislike for?"

"You're putting words into my mouth."

"What then? Explain. I really want to know."

"You're phony."

She hadn't intended for it to come out quite like that, but he'd pushed, and suddenly it was said. He stiffened, and the edge came off the smile.

"What makes you say that? I've admitted I don't know anything about living here. What's phony about that?"

She couldn't quite look him in the eye. "Maybe 'phony' isn't the right word," she admitted. "But you just don't add up. For one thing, your clothes are all new, like your regular wardrobe just wouldn't have worked. Then there's that landing you made earlier. I'd bet you haven't done it too many times before, not on a lake, anyway. And another thing, why come way up here? There are bound to be lots of other jobs, better jobs, back in Illinois or wherever."

"That's it?" he asked. "New clothes, a bobbled landing, and the fact that there are other jobs in this world? That's what makes you act like an untamed animal around me?"

Laney bristled. "I do not!"

"I think you do," he shot back, stepping closer. "I think I make you feel skittish and nervous, maybe even a little excited."

"I don't know what you're talking about!"

"Don't you?" he countered, and he reached out with his right hand, fingers pointed downward, and covered the spot on her now-clean thigh where he had wiped it. Scalded, she careened away, back and to the side, her shoulder coming up hard against the doorjamb and the wall. He followed instantly, stepping forward.

She gasped, stunned by the electrical impact and supremely aware of his nearness.

"You trembled before when I touched you." His voice was deep and soft and rumbling, his eyes dark and glistening. She lifted a hand to her glossy hair. Had she actually trembled? She shuddered now, remembering the chill that had chased up her spine, feeling her heart pound and her eyes grow wide. "It's called physical attraction," he said quietly. "I felt it the moment I saw you."

Her mouth dropped open, not because of what he'd said or even what he'd done, but because of her reaction to it. *This has happened before,* a voice said inside her head. It *had* happened before. Other men had made similar passes at her, and when they had, she had been cool and—angry.

By rote, she heard herself saying words she'd said before, making gestures that were rehearsed. A kind of relief swept through her along with the strengthening anger. "I'll thank you to keep your hands to yourself." She straightened her back, squared her shoulders and dropped her chin. "And believe me, if you don't, I'll make you wish you had. If you touch me again, I'll break your arm."

"Oh, I don't think you'd do that," he replied softly, and his hand fluttered somewhere near her ear. She slapped it away, and those dark brows shot upward. He turned his head slightly, eyeing her.

"I mean it," she stated flatly. "That might be hard for an arrogant, conceited idiot like you to understand, but that's the..."

"How old are you?" he asked abruptly, throwing her off balance again.

"What? Twenty-three, but don't change the..."

"Really?" He interrupted again, flashing that irrepressible grin. "I thought you might be younger than that."

For the second time in two minutes, her mouth dropped open. Her hands went automatically to her hips. "*Younger!* What do I look like to you, a *child*?"

"Hardly that," he said, laughing. "How long have you lived here?"

She blinked at him. Now what did *that* have to do with anything? "I was born right here in this house."

"You're kidding."

"Hardly that," she mimicked sarcastically.

He refused to be offended. "No, really. You mean to tell me you've lived here all your life?"

"All twenty-three years and five months."

"But where did you go to school?"

"In my mother's kitchen," she told him, her light eyes daring him to make some clever remark about that. He got the message clearly enough. He compressed his mouth over words he was obviously reconsidering, and his hand smoothed through his hair from his temple to his nape, managing somehow not to disturb the part.

"Sounds as if you've had an unusual life," he commented carefully, and Laney felt herself beginning to relax.

"I think so."

"And you don't regret it, being so isolated, I mean."

"Why should I?"

He shrugged. "I don't know, but I can't help wondering what an attractive young woman like you finds to do with herself out here."

Laney stiffened again, angry that she'd allowed him this opening, and curled her slender fingers into fists. "Not that it's any of your business," she said caustically, "but I do just about what any young man my age would do. I hunt. I fish. I'm one of the best damned trackers in these mountains, and I have a license to prove it. Besides that, I do my share of the work around here, hard work. It's more than enough to fill anybody's days."

"And the nights?" he asked softly, and it seemed to Laney that the little distance between them shrank. She lifted her chin defensively and made her voice strong and level.

"The nights I spend reading or talking with my mother. Sometimes I play chess with my father, and sometimes I go up to Crater's." The expression on his face sharpened, or was that her imagination?

"Who or what is Crater?" he asked, and something in his voice sent a tiny surge of satisfaction through her. She shifted her weight, her feet set wide apart, her arms folded against her slender middle, her gaze level and steady.

"He's a special friend of mine," she said pointedly. "He lives on the mountain and likes his privacy, if you know what I mean."

"He's a hermit of sorts?"

"Not exactly. He's a genuine mountain man, lives like people did a hundred years ago. Let's just say he doesn't take kindly to strangers."

She smiled to herself, thinking of what Crater might do should Danzer Wilson be stupid enough to go calling. As if reading her thoughts, the handsome face before her seemed suddenly to close in on itself, to harden.

"He's not the only one," said Danzer cryptically. "You two must get along real well."

"As a matter of fact, we do," she retorted, "and you're certainly not the one to change that."

He glared at her. "You're just not going to loosen up even a little bit, are you? No matter what I say or do, you've made up your mind about me, and you're just not going to change it."

"Why should I?" she shot back, and he shook his head, eyes and mouth wide.

"You're about the unfriendliest person I've ever met," he pronounced. "Bar none."

"You're no charmer yourself," she flung back at him, "and I've had enough of this." Coolly, she stepped through the door and slammed it.

For a moment, she stood there, imagining the look of shock on his face. Then the raspy sound of his near-silent laughter assaulted her, and she whirled away, gritting her teeth.

She hadn't been wrong about him. Her instincts were right on target. He didn't belong. Danzer Wilson was trouble that had dropped out of the sky, change on the wind, and it wouldn't be long before everyone knew it.

Danzer spent the majority of the next two weeks with Hiram Scott. It wasn't difficult. Hi was a quiet man but not an antisocial one. Dan quickly learned not to force the conversation, and the two became amiable companions. He knew Hiram liked him; the natural manner in which the older man included Danzer in his normal activities made that obvious, and Danzer was grateful. After the way he had mishandled Laney, he knew he would need all the friends he could get just to stay on here. In fact, he half expected to be handed his walking papers that very first afternoon, but Laney apparently said nothing to her parents about the dumb pass he'd made at her. And dumb was the word for it, all right.

He'd been dumb as stone to think she'd been somehow moved by his wiping fish gunk all over her jeans. That male ego of his was truly getting out of hand. Her hostility had been palpable, evident enough to embarrass both her parents and make him especially aware of her. Yet the first moment he'd gotten her alone, he'd made a pass. He hadn't even considered there might be a boyfriend. The prospect of having a social life out here in the wilderness had seemed unlikely at best, but then he'd realized that he didn't know up from down out here. This was not the Chicago business world. He couldn't go around making snap assessments of—or passes at—attractive women. Not smart. Considering the trouble he'd gone to just to work out this arrangement, not smart at all.

Anyway, what did it matter whether the daughter liked him or not, as long as the father did? Hi was the one with the power to deny him this experience. She was just a kid, for Pete's sake. Well, all right, twenty-three wasn't juvenile, but emotionally she was probably thirteen. This Crater guy was probably the only boyfriend she'd ever had. Besides, she wasn't *that* good-looking. It was just part of the fantasy, the excitement of transmuting a dream into reality. She was his "wilderness woman." When he got to the Caribbean expedition, there would undoubtedly be some legendary Honduran beauty there to greet him. Not that this was about women, not at all. This was about fulfillment, about making life rich and exciting. God knew he'd been bored out of his gourd for the last five years.

The first few years out of college had been exciting and challenging. He'd worked like a madman to get to the top of his profession, and at twenty-nine had been one of the youngest investment bankers ever to sit at the helm of an international consortium. But that old homily about there being nowhere to go from the top but down was true, and now he wondered what he was going to do with the rest of his life. It was as if he'd expended the struggle of a lifetime in those first hectic years, and now he didn't care to repeat the process. He couldn't put his finger on it, but something was missing. He'd made his fortune, and then everyone had told him what he needed was a challenge. So, he'd gone after the biggest deal of his career. Now, thanks largely to him, the first autos were about to roll off the production line at a new Japanese/American plant in northern Mexico, financed by a complicated coalition of Arab, French, German and Danish banks. He'd made a fat percentage as a finder's fee on the foreign-loan package, and his own bank had won a hefty, heavily guaranteed portion of the deal, out of which he'd been awarded a substantial bonus.

He now had funds in six of the world's finest financial institutions, and his overall feeling about the whole thing was one of utter emptiness. Increasingly he felt like a stranger in a strange world. When he'd first broached the subject of resigning with his two most trusted high-level executives, they'd begged him to reconsider. Once word had leaked out, some members of the board had made veiled threats of scandal and lawsuit, not that he cared a whit about that. No one had anything on him because there was nothing to have; he'd made sure of it. But it was true that any shake-up in management of a successful financial business was bound to have negative results initially, and Danzer did feel an obligation to the stockholders. So they'd worked out a deal for a year long sabbatical, a vacation from reality, and with the first real excitement he'd felt in a long time, he'd set about planning what he was going to do with that time.

He had the money to indulge himself and no personal obligations to get in the way. He'd spent nine months working out the details, and he'd been as quiet about it as he could. He wanted to experience other people's lives for a while, see what made them more satisfying then his own. His dream: modern-day mountain man. After that would come three months at sea with New Guinea the eventual destination, a safari across the African continent, and a stint diving for sunken treasure off the coast of Honduras. Whenever one dream bogged down in the sediment of day-to-day living, he would have the allure or the memory of another to buoy his spirits and fire his imagination.

Maybe in the end he'd write a book about it all and discover a hidden talent to be pursued with renewed passion. Maybe he'd be just as jaded and discontented as before. And maybe he'd find that indefinable something that made a man as content as Hiram Scott was in his beautiful valley. All he knew was that there had to be more to life than sitting behind the biggest desk in the office. If only he knew what that was....

The first days in Montana weren't particularly exciting, but they were full and *different*. His very first afternoon, Hi began teaching him to recognize the variety of fish found in the lakes and streams, the quotas allowed and the manners in which each could be legally taken. They spent one entire evening looking over Hi's handmade lure collection. The next morning and every one thereafter, the two men chopped wood. Hi was pleased to find Dan's back strong and his mind quick to grasp the technique of chopping and splitting the logs to the necessary lengths. It was hot work, and less than an hour of it would have Danzer stripped to the waist and contemplating a dip in the lake. There was never time for it, though, and after a few days he changed his mind about that swim altogether.

It was around five o'clock in the afternoon one day when Hi decided it was time to get in a little practice with those lures they'd studied in such intimate detail. They went out into the lake in a canoe, not expecting even to catch anything, but simply to practice. After several disappointing nibbles, however, Dan felt a terrific drag on the line. He'd hooked what felt like the great-granddaddy of them all. He fought that freshwater whale for what seemed like a quarter of an hour but was more probably about three minutes. Then, an impatient yank snapped the line where it joined the hook, and the resulting backlash rocked the canoe so hard both men went right over the edge into water so frigid Dan's teeth chattered hard enough, it seemed, to break his jaw.

Hi was downright mad at first, but thankfully his fishing gear was saved, and by the time they got back to the house, he was in a good enough mood to rib Danzer and regale his wife with a hilarious account of the whole incident. Lil made a fresh pot of coffee and spiked it with brandy, so that by the time Danzer had warmed up to a toasty fire he was also relaxed and mellow enough not to be disturbed by Laney's scowling presence. His belly full of Lil's venison stew and several cups of strong black coffee liberally laced, he'd gone to bed early and slept like a baby.

Morning brought him a mild headache and enough sore muscles to make a less fit man stay in bed groaning. But he hauled out and performed a few stretching exercises to limber up, glad to see that the soreness was lessening day by day. Hi seemed completely unaffected by the previous day's activities, so Dan relaxed and tried harder than ever to make himself useful.

He helped Hi repair the roof of the low, divided shed out back where he kept his fishing gear and hides, watching with something approaching awe as the older man split replacement shingles out of a specially selected and properly aged log. Later they tinkered with the generators, and Hi showed him a fine meadow where they could cut grass for the milk cow and calf.

There was always plenty of work, but Hi managed to find a good bit of leisure time. They played chess and checkers and cards, swapped tall tales, and spent time simply talking. One day they hiked around the lake to fish from its far bank, admiring the impressive home Hiram and Lillian had made for themselves. Danzer listened with humble admiration as Hi told him unabashedly how he'd built this place, inch by inch, with his own two hands, how he'd cleared the land, how he'd chosen, felled, stripped, hauled, cut, notched, stacked and mortared the logs, then done much the same with the rock. He talked about making his own brick and splitting flags and towing the windows and generators and plumbing pipe upriver by barge, about how he'd had to tear down the first fireplace and start over—with winter creeping down the mountainside toward them and Lil sick with the early stages of pregnancy and their money all gone and no prospect of more until the end of trapping season. He told it all with a minimum of words, and Danzer had to wonder if simple things weren't somehow magnified out here and made more than they were in the everyday world.

Hi's amazing tale left Danzer feeling full and contemplative, and Hiram himself seemed in a reflective, solitary mood, so by silent, mutual consent, they went their separate ways afterward. Dan decided it was a good time to service and pamper the plane. It could have waited until morning, but he wanted something to do with his hands. He needed accomplishment, tangible results, but when he went out, Laney was there on the pier silently and sullenly cleaning the string of trout he and Hi had caught and carried home. He spoke, but she merely glared in return. There was something about that woman that cut him to the quick, and try as he might, he couldn't ignore her.

As it was, he couldn't quite concentrate on the work. Everything checked out okay with the engine and controls, and it was a small matter to fill the tank from one of the two drums of fuel he'd flown in with him and then to load the empty into the special rack he'd had built in the small cargo hold. But she took her jolly good time over those fish, unnerving him to the point where he made a mess of waxing and polishing the exterior, so much so that he was ashamed to leave it and go inside when darkness made it impossible to continue rewaxing. He couldn't help wondering if she'd noticed, but that evening at the dinner table, she neither spoke nor glanced in his direction, giving no indication that she even recognized his existence, let alone took satisfaction in his small failures.

That night, he didn't sleep well at all, though he was achingly tired and desperately needed to be fresh for the next day's flight. What troubled him was not just the feeling of smallness that Hi's tale of building had produced in him, for he was wise enough to know that his own accomplishments had been real and sustaining in ways he could not see from behind the stacks of papers on his desk. It was more than that. It was the utter contempt he sensed in the girl. No one had felt that way about him before, no one he knew of, and he didn't like it, couldn't shake it. It ate at him, taunted him, and after the things he'd said to her, the embarrassing incident with Hi on the river, the way he'd muffed a simple wax job, and the deep feeling of dissatisfaction he'd brought with him to this place, he was beginning to wonder if Laney possessed some special vision that allowed her to see in him what no one else had ever seen, that great, grating uncertainty that made his life so meaningless, so dull, so puzzling.

Early the next morning Danzer went over his charts and flight path with Hiram, pleased in spite of himself to be knowledgeable about something that was a mystery to the older man. Hiram was an apt pupil and proved to be of help with the topographical charts, describing in detail what landmarks he might be able to spot from the air. He gave Danzer the appropriate call letters and frequency for making contact by shortwave radio with the parents of the children he was going to pick up in Miles City. Their grandfather, whom Hi called Bill Denton, was a rancher and Lil's cousin. His children had spent happy weeks at the lodge, providing companionship for Laney. Now his grandchildren paid a long visit every summer, allowing everyone a break from the routine. Danzer sensed it was more for Lil's enjoyment than anything else.

He felt certain he could find Miles City without trouble. Barring unforeseen troubles, he should be back at the lodge with the children before nightfall. If for some reason he was delayed beyond that, he would contact them via shortwave.

The trip was a nightmare. He had no trouble finding Miles City or hooking up with the Dentons. They were a nice young couple, and the kids, Kevin and Annie, seemed well behaved, but they were all a bit uneasy about that plane trip. Mrs. Denton cried when her children boarded, and that set little Annie to blubbering, causing Danzer to unload them again and treat the pair to sodas and ice cream bars while he charmed and teased smiles from the female faction. The ice cream was a big mistake, as he was to find out when it was too late.

In the proper mood now, he ushered the little ones into their seats, buckled them in and gave each a pat on their heads. Annie smiled up at him trustingly, and it was the last time he was to see such an expression for the remainder of the trip. Miles City had hardly disappeared behind them when she began to spew ice cream and cola all over the place. Unable to leave the controls himself, he had to instruct the boy how to care for her. At nine, he was an unusually resourceful child, but Annie's air sickness proved stubborn and severe. She begged to go home, and Kevin begged to go on. In the end, Annie wound up in the copilot's seat, barfing all over the controls, while Kevin held his nose in the rear section and made gagging sounds, and Danzer tried to be sympathetic without crashing them into a mountainside. By the time they reached the lodge, he was questioning his sanity for deciding to inflict such an experience on himself and two innocent children. Only Lil's confident, comforting care and Hi's steady clap on the shoulder made him feel he'd actually done the best he could in a bad situation.

That night, with both children fully recovered and talking excitedly about hunting and fishing and hiking, and Lil so obviously happy to have them there, and everyone else's attention centering on the kids, Danzer had a chance to really study Laney. She'd rolled her eyes and thrown up her hands when he'd disembarked with little Annie in his arms, both of them smelly and soiled. But her concern for the sick child left her no time to do more than send a single, accusing glare in his direction. He'd noted a smug smile or two since then, but, as usual, she'd said not a word to him. Lying on her belly on a big bearskin rug before the fire in the great room, she arm-wrestled with the boy and let him beat her, then told a fine, improbable tale about an eighteen-point buck she'd seen last deer season.

Dan sat on the wide rock ledge that ran around the room, his back to the wall, and watched her. She was no product of his imagination, and if her surroundings so complemented her beauty as to enhance it, he couldn't imagine surroundings that would not. She was slim and fit and graceful and shaped with womanly fullness in all the right places. Her hair was long and thick and glossy, the kind of brown one finds in fine woods, expensive leathers and rich furs, not too dark and not too light, with coppery highlights that set it afire against the sun. Her skin was clear and smooth, her features regular but distinctive, her lips full and red, and her eyes large and round and a bright, light green, like clear, mossy pools on a cloudless day. Her ears were small and her chin stubborn, her neck long and slender, her voice low and husky. Without cosmetics or stylish clothing, without even the barest feminine accoutrements, she was, like her mother, beautiful. And she was so womanly she made him ache.

He thought of Lil with respect and growing affection devoid of desire or embarrassment. He ought to be able to think of Laney dispassionately, considering her opinion of him. He ought not to think of her as desirable and female. But there she lay, laughing with that boy, lovely and soft and compelling—and filled with disdain for him. He made up his mind then and there that it was going to change. He didn't know how he was going to do it yet, but he'd change her mind about him, one way or another.

Chapter Three

 Dad, you can't be serious."

Laney put both hands on her hips and looked down at her father. He grunted and pulled on a boot. Bending over from his seat on the foot of his bed, he began to thread the laces through the steel-rimmed eyes.

"It's just when he's flying the kids," he said, his concentration still on his boots, and Laney threw up her hands.

"He shouldn't be flying anyone anywhere! After he brought those poor children back here sick and trembling, I thought you'd see this whole thing was a mistake!"

He tied the laces together and pulled his pant leg down over the top of the boot before straightening to study his daughter. "I don't get you on this, Laney," he said. "The way I see it, we should have figured—both of us—that he'd need help with the kids. He figured it'd be okay 'cause he'd taken up his nieces before and they'd loved it. How was I to know what could happen? But now we both know, and the only logical thing to do is to send someone with him when there's kids along. I don't see what's to get upset about.''

"I don't see why we need to be bothering with all this in the first place!'' she declared.

"Laney, if you can't see this is easier on everybody than travelin' the river, then you've got real brain trouble. We've had kids get sick in canoes before, *and* scared *and* wet. Heck, we've had full-grown men hang over the side the whole dang trip. This way is faster and at least as safe. I can't believe you're scared to fly 'cause I've seen you do things that turned my skin cold. So what is your problem?''

"I just don't like it,'' she insisted. "I don't want to go with him, and I don't think it's going to work out well for us.''

Hiram Scott sighed and bent over his second boot. "Well, I don't know when you stopped trustin' my judgment on these things or why you've decided to make it harder than it has to be, but if that's how you feel . . .''

"That's not fair, Dad.'' She brushed her hair off her shoulders with both hands. "I've always had confidence in you. It's him I don't trust.''

He pushed his foot into the second boot. "Now that makes no sense at all. Dan's an upstandin' fellow. He's no mountain man, but then again he doesn't claim to be. He's just a man doin' a job and samplin' a different way of life in the process. Nothin' wrong with that.''

"But, Dad, he doesn't belong here.''

"Nobody said he did, but what's that got to do with the price of beans?''

"How can I make you understand?'' she asked, pushing her fingers into her temples.

"You can't make me understand because it don't make sense,'' he said, wrapping his shoelaces twice around his ankle before tying them together. "If you won't go, then your mother and I will work it out between us, but that seems foolish when you could do it so easily."

Laney made a face, feeling guilty and petty and right all at the same time. "I didn't say I *wouldn't* go," she grumbled, "I said I didn't want to."

"Well, it's your decision," he said lightly, and Laney knew *he* knew she was capitulating. She bit her lip and suppressed the urge to stomp her foot.

"I'll go," she said reluctantly, "but I don't like it."

He shrugged and folded his pant leg down. "Up to you."

She rolled her eyes. "I said I'd go!"

He sat up and grinned at her. "You're not nearly as stubborn as your mama says you are."

Laney glared at him, then saw the twinkle in his eye and could not stop herself from responding to it. "I am so, and you know it," she insisted, a smile sneaking up on her.

"All right, have it your way," he teased, standing up.

Laney punched him playfully on the shoulder. "Guess I'll have it *your* way this time."

He laughed and threw an arm around her neck, hugging her in a hammerlock. "You're a good girl," he said, "and I'm betting you're gonna like flyin' around up there with the little birdies."

"I may like flying around with the birdies," she said, wrapping her arms about his waist, "but I'm not going to like flying around with Danzer Wilson."

He kissed her on the top of her head and let her go. She dropped her arms. "Don't underestimate him, Laney. That's more man than you're used to."

"He's not more man than you," she said. He laughed.

"True enough! Now go help your ma rustle me up a tall stack of griddle cakes. I'm man enough to eat a mountain this morning."

She pecked a kiss on his stubbly cheek and hurried away, glad as always to have pleased him, despite her misgivings about flying off into the wild blue yonder with handsome, mysterious Danzer Wilson.

She closed the door to her parents' bedroom and moved down the narrow hallway, away from the bath at the far end, toward the kitchen. She loved this part of the house. Her parents' bedroom was only slightly larger than the others, but it was also the only one with a double bed or a real closet built into one corner. It was cozy and private and made her feel safe and small and special. She still remembered the long-ago times when she had slept in a little lean-to where the bathroom now stood and listened to the comforting sounds of her parents next door, talking together in that special way of all lovers. It had made her feel part of a warm, happy unit.

In fact, she had always felt that way, with two or three memorable exceptions, such as the time of the earthquake scare. The ground had trembled day after day, and her father, fearing a repeat of the 1959 disaster during which dozens of campers were killed and several others were stranded in high mountain country, had insisted she and her mother go to stay with family in Canada until the threat of a major quake was past. They'd been apart for weeks, and though she would later happily stay away on long family visits, it had felt at the time as if their very way of life was threatened.

It had felt much the same way for several days a few years later when her parents had simply stopped talking to each other. She'd known even then that they had fought over something; she was never to know about what, but her little girl's mind had imagined a rift in the relationship that might never be mended. She still remembered the relief she'd felt when she'd walked into the kitchen one day and found them standing there in each other's arms. She remembered, too, the way her mother had sung softly to herself for many mornings afterward and the happy, secretive smiles her father had worn.

Now she felt threatened again, and she didn't know why or how, only that it had to do with a sense of change and a tall, dark man who made her feel itchy all over in a way she couldn't describe. Perhaps it had to do with more than that. Perhaps it had to do with thoughts she'd had recently of life outside their private valley or with the odd, nameless, melancholy longings that came over her every so often and left her feeling lonely and vaguely disloyal. Perhaps it had to do with the fact that she had begun to wonder what her future might hold when her parents were gone and she was left alone here with only the mountains for company. But if it had to do with any of those things, she wasn't ready to fully admit that. All she knew was that she had felt a mild restlessness and a mysterious anxiety, as if change were already in the air, and then there had come a call on the radio and talk of airplanes and convenience where none had been sought before. Even before she'd seen him, Laney had felt Danzer Wilson was a threat. Now she knew. She didn't understand, but she knew, and she could only wonder why her father didn't feel the threat, too.

Laney passed the wide entry into the great room and stepped into the kitchen. The floor here was slightly lower than that in the hallway, but Laney had negotiated it for so long that she didn't even break stride. The room was quite small, two steps from the doorway to the end of the table, two more to the sink, and four from the table to the stove on one end and the cellar on the other. Her mother had already brought up a silver gallon can of syrup and was now pouring saucer-size pancakes onto the heavy iron griddle placed over two gas burners on the front of her stove. Laney went over and gave her a kiss on the cheek.

"Your husband says he's man enough to eat a whole mountain of griddle cakes."

"Oh, he does, does he?" Lillian laughed and set down the batter bowl to take up a spatula. The first ones were almost ready to turn. "Well, I guess I better get busy then. Between him and Danzer and those babies, I'm going to be here right on into lunchtime. Set the big table, dear, and bring up one of those little kegs of apple juice, not cider, mind you, but juice. Dan has a special liking for that sweet juice and I'm afraid the cider would be too bitter with that syrup."

Laney halted as she reached for a set of chipped blue plates on the shelves mounted on the wall to the side of the sink. Danzer Wilson again. Now her mother was actually catering to him.

"Papa likes cranberry, doesn't he, Mama?" she asked innocently.

"Yes," her mother agreed absently, flipping the last of the griddle cakes. That done, she immediately began taking up the first. "But he likes apple, too, and since it's a special favorite of Dan's..."

"I don't see what Danzer Wilson's favorites have to do with anything," Laney interrupted moodily. "He's just hired help, for goodness' sake, and not very good help at that."

"Why, Laney!" Lillian turned around, spatula in hand. "How can you say that? He's made things so much easier on everyone, and he's such good company for your father."

"It seems to me he's just complicated things," Laney argued, "and I can't for the life of me see what you and Dad see in him."

Lillian's mouth dropped open. "Why, there's lots to like about Dan. He's witty and interesting and capable. Your dad says he listens and learns fast, and he's not too proud to say he doesn't know a thing when he doesn't. And I, for one, am resting a lot easier just knowing he's cut the work load around here."

"We were doing just fine without him," Laney insisted petulantly. "Dad and I have been riding the river every season for fifteen years."

"And it's time your father started slowing down, Laney, so what do you propose we do, stop taking hunting parties altogether? I see this as a good compromise. If it works out, we can hire someone else next year, maybe someone permanent. That way Hi can keep on for a few more seasons."

"Mother!" Laney was shocked and angry. "How can you say that? You talk like Dad's an old man!"

Lillian gave her daughter a pitying look and said softly, "He's not young anymore, sweetie, and he knows it."

Laney stared at her. For the first time, she really saw the fine lines around her mother's eyes and the one or two silvery hairs at her temples. How old was her mother, forty-seven, forty-eight? And her father would be fifty-five, not old by any means, but not young anymore, either.

"Laney," her mother said at last, "hasn't it ever occurred to you that your father might like to put his feet up for a change and just sit by the fire? It's a hard life out here, a good one but hard, and he's started thinking about the time when he can take things a little easier."

"He can take things easier now," Laney insisted. "I can take over—"

"No," Lillian said flatly, her voice growing quietly fierce. "For you as well as for him."

Laney's eyes grew wide. "Mother, I always thought, I always assumed the time would come when I would take over the heavier responsibilities."

"No," Lillian said again. "He doesn't want that. I don't want that. It's time you started thinking about making your own life, just as we made ours. If it's here in these mountains, fine, but it has to be for you, not for us. Your dad's pride won't allow for anything else, nor my good sense."

Laney realized there were tears in her mother's eyes. "Oh, Mama," she said, stepping forward to put her arms around her mother. Lillian stood a moment, her head on her daughter's shoulders, then she sniffed loudly and turned away to pour more griddle cakes.

"Don't put blame, Laney," she counseled gently. "Time passes of its own accord."

"I won't, Mama," she answered, her voice little more than a whisper, and they both knew who it was Lillian wanted to protect from unjust blame. "I'll lay the table now."

She brought the plates down and slipped quickly from the room, her mind full of all her mother had said. As she arranged the big blue plates around one end of the long, narrow table, she heard footsteps on the landing above and the laughter of small voices. She turned to see Danzer Wilson coming down the stairs with two giggling bundles hanging around his neck. He pretended to be staggering under their weight at first, then suddenly straightened and, with an arm around each, dashed down the steps. There were screams and peals of laughter, and at the bottom of the stairs hugs and noisy smacks from Annie, while Kevin danced about, whooping. Danzer gave each head an affectionate rub and answered such questions as, "How'd you get so strong?" and "Can you teach me to fly a plane?"

Laney turned away. The children had quickly forgotten yesterday's unpleasant experience in the air and found a genuine liking for Danzer Wilson. He'd been good with them, and she had to admit he hadn't been the bother these past weeks she'd expected. He'd been a lot of help, in fact, and he hadn't uttered even one belligerent or baiting word. He'd taken the ribbing about tipping into the lake good-naturedly and proved an apt student to boot.

All right, she told herself sternly, *changes come when no one's to blame. You don't have to like him, but you can at least be polite.* It wasn't as if she actually *dis*liked him, at least not anymore. Still, Laney Scott did not always capitulate so easily as her father made it seem. Danzer Wilson was an outsider, a stranger still, and she was not going to let herself forget that. Maybe the problem was that she didn't know him well enough. Maybe, she mused, if she got to know him better she could put to rest what troubled her about him. That, she decided, was what she must do, like it or not. She laid the last plate and went back to the kitchen for flatware, telling herself that the thrill of excitement she felt had to do with anticipation of her first plane ride, now that it was certain, rather than anything to do with the pilot—and she even believed it.

Laney tapped her foot impatiently as she waited for Danzer to finish his checklist. In the last half hour he'd crawled all over his small craft, probing, wiping, tightening. He'd filled the fuel tank with the use of a hand pump, which he'd then cleaned and dried meticulously before putting it away, all the while ignoring her as if she didn't exist. She'd cleared her throat, shuffled her feet, kicked a small rock off the pier into the lake, but if he even knew she was there, he gave no sign. It had been that way for days, and her patience was about at its end. She'd tried to be fair. It wasn't her fault if they couldn't be friends. It just proved what she'd felt all along.

She gritted her teeth, feeling the fool as she remembered how she'd tried to approach him, pouring his coffee, offering him seconds before he'd even finished the first, joining uninvited in the play when he was romping with the kids, challenging him to a game of chess only to have him decline, and then having to sit through a losing match with her father while her attention was elsewhere. He'd acted as if she were part of the furniture most of the time, and when it was absolutely necessary to speak, he'd done so with distant courtesy. No one had ever ignored her so politely, and it was positively unnerving. Sometimes she almost believed he was doing it on purpose.

Once, while fishing off the dock with her father and Danzer, she'd actually pulled an eight-inch-long trout out of the water and plopped it into his lap. He'd calmly captured it with his hands, removed the hook, strung it, and turned back to his own pole without a word, making a long, perfect cast into the middle of the lake. She'd wanted to knock him into the water, but then she'd caught a glimpse of her father's face. He'd tried to hide the knowing smile, but the sharpness about his eyes had left no doubt that he knew what she'd been doing. She'd felt her face go crimson, and both had turned quickly away, while Danzer had sat there oblivious to it all. And now here they were, playing the same old game, she trying subtly to attract his attention, he as unaware as the rock she'd kicked into the lake. It seemed he'd turned the tables on her, but she couldn't honestly say he'd tried to get her attention after the fiasco of that first day. He was a hard one to figure, Danzer Wilson. She gave it up and stood quietly while he completed his routine.

In a few moments, he straightened and wiped his hands on a dull red cloth. For the first time he seemed to notice her. She was torn between a smile and scowl, then she heard the footsteps behind her and glanced over her shoulder, realizing his notice was not for her but for her parents and the children. The kids ran forward and past her, calling his name. He went down on one knee to dispense hugs as her parents came up beside her.

"Annie and Kevin wanted to say goodbye," Lillian announced, threading her arm about her daughter's waist.

"You've got to take me up in that thing sometime, Dan," Hiram said, hooking his thumbs in his hip pockets. Danzer looked up and smiled.

"Anytime."

"Maybe when you get back. You and Laney better get going now."

Lillian gave Laney a squeeze and lifted a hand in farewell to Dan. Hiram called the kids, and they reluctantly backed away. Dan stood and for the first time in a long while made direct eye contact with Laney. To her surprise, he smiled softly, genuinely, and she felt a surge of pleasure. She stepped forward, and he took her hand, helping her up into the craft. Moments later, she was buckled into her seat beside him in the cockpit, listening to the chug of the engine as they taxied out into the center of the lake.

"Ready?" he asked, and she turned to face him, nodding. "Here we go."

He pushed the throttle forward, and the plane picked up speed, going faster and faster until the force of the thrust pinned her in her seat. She hardly felt the lift-off. One moment the world was whizzing by her, and the next, it was falling away behind.

They banked slowly against the big sky and passed over the lodge below. Laney waved to the tiny figures of her parents and the even smaller ones of the children, and then they were gone. Moments later the valley, too, was far away, and the lowest peaks of the mountains were passing below them. They climbed again, and Laney watched, mesmerized, as they lifted into the white froth of a cloud. She caught her breath, craning her neck in every direction to see as much as she could. White cliffs upon which she had stood after exhausting days of climbing now broke through the clouds below and drifted gently away. She marveled at how little effort it took for her to soar above them, and when she looked at Danzer, she found him watching her and smiling as if quite pleased with himself.

"Having fun?" he asked, shifting his gaze straight ahead.

"Yes," she admitted. "I didn't know it would be like this."

He nodded. "I know what you mean. Nothing I had imagined really prepared me for the kind of life you lead."

She turned away, fascinated by the view and not entirely mollified by his sudden interest after days of being ignored. Two could play his game. The clouds slowly dissipated. Only wisps of gossamer and distant cotton puffs remained. The peaks and valleys below were painted in deep, rich colors and clean, frosty white. The pines and firs carpeted the lower slopes in darkest green. Above them ran striated, uneven lines of mottled browns and grays, topped with the ragged crests of glistening white. Far below and in vivid streams were pools and streaks of bright blue water sparkling shreds and drops of silver in the yellow sunlight. It was more beautiful than she had realized.

"Fascinating, isn't it?" he said, and she replied with an absent murmur.

"No pictures I've ever seen did justice to it," he went on, and this time she made no reply at all. Several minutes passed in silence, and Laney stared so hard through the glass that she became unaware of it. It was as if she were floating all alone far above the earth. Eventually he called her back.

"Do you know the town where we're heading?" he asked. "We'll want something to eat before we start back."

She nodded and hummed a positive reply, eyes glued on a large bird circling far ahead and below them. A bit later he tried again.

"Do you know these kids? They're sons of friends of yours, aren't they?" She gave him a preoccupied nod. "They must be older than you." She felt that obvious enough not to require an answer. "We'll be there soon," he went on, but she already knew that, for they were leaving the mountains and heading northeast into the plains.

She was amazed at how far she could see. There were patchwork fields and large, irregular swatches of pale grass broken by dark, squiggly lines of trees along a creek bank or around a small splotch of blue water. She saw no structures, but as they dropped lower, she could make out the tiny, moving figure of an occasional cow and, once, what seemed to be a moose. She spotted something moving, and after several intense moments of study, she realized it was a pickup truck tearing along a dirt road so narrow she couldn't see it for the grass until they were right over the top of it.

Laney truly was fascinated by the view, so much so that it was harder to pay attention to what Dan was saying than to ignore him. So, other than a vague impression of a change in the background noise, she really didn't hear the question. Then suddenly the earth tilted away and the sky rolled up in its place. For one heart-stopping moment she was completely disoriented, and the next she knew she was upside down, the belt across her lap cutting into the tops of her legs, her hair hanging "up" instead of what it should have been—down. Without realizing what she was doing, she had reached across the cockpit and grasped the top of Danzer's shoulder. Now she turned her head that way, dismayed by the extra effort it took to do so. He cut his eyes at her, a wide, teeth-baring grin in place, and the next instant her hair was falling down around her head and the horizon had rolled around into its proper realm.

"You did that on purpose!" she accused him, pushing her hair off her face.

"I thought you'd like a little thrill," he said through his grin. "Ready for the next one?"

Before she could speak, he pulled the plane into a hard dive, pushing her heart up into her throat. She fixed her eyes on the ground coming up fast in front of them, and in her head a voice was saying, "Any second now. Any second, he'll pull up." She clenched her teeth to keep from calling out, and just when she couldn't bear to look anymore, the edge of the sky pushed down into view. The force of the turn pinned her to her seat, and then, quite against her will, she leaned over onto her side, the earth to her right, the sky to her left. Whirling in that limbo between earth and sky, she felt a surge of exaltation, a fascination that forced laughter up inside her. The plane banked to the left, and she released the exhilaration, laughter spilling out into the cockpit. They climbed high, almost straight up, it seemed, and then banked wildly to the left, spiraling downward in ever-widening loops, leveling out finally well above the ground.

The laughter had dwindled as the loops widened, bringing them slowly back to the now-mundane business of getting where they were going. But Laney could not suppress a smile. He grinned at her, and she reached over to give him a playful shove on the shoulder.

"You could have killed us, you idiot!"

"But it was fun, wasn't it?"

She couldn't be angry, and she couldn't be stern, so she just gave up and was happy. "I wasn't really frightened," she told him, "just shocked. I could tell you were in control."

He smiled at her, and something electric and alive passed between them. The smile faded into softness. "I have to tell you," he said. "You're the most naturally beautiful woman I've ever seen."

She held his eyes for an instant longer, a new kind of thrill sweeping over her and leaving a flush in its wake. She dropped her gaze, feeling the color blossom on her cheeks. She took a breath then and thanked him, awkwardness overtaking her.

He looked away and changed the subject abruptly. This time she made an effort to reply, and soon the awkwardness evaporated as the conversation became real and intent. They talked about flying and different aircraft and about living in relative isolation and their respective childhoods. They talked through the remainder of the trip, and on the ground once more they talked through a late lunch of burgers and chips. Then, finding they were late for the rendezvous, he took her hand and pulled her along at a run, as if she couldn't have kept up on her own, so that when they met the Pettys, they were hand-in-hand and laughing too hard to catch their breath.

It was good to see old friends like Jerry and Susan Petty. Jerry had come to the lodge as a boy of twelve with a hunting party that included his father. A six-year-old tomboy, Laney had first made a nuisance of herself and then become an adoring surrogate sister. Jerry and his father had returned each year for several years, and then, newly married, Jerry had returned on his own. The next year at Lillian's insistence, he'd brought a pregnant Susan with him. Since then, Lillian had taken it upon herself to provide a couple of peaceful weeks of vacation from parenthood for the Pettys, and they looked forward to those times as only the parents of three little boys born within four years could do.

Laney herded Mark and Matthew, aged nine and eight respectively, toward the plane, while Danzer carried six-year-old Mike piggyback. She helped Danzer belt them in, taking the fourth chair for herself, and was impressed with the manner in which Danzer commanded their attention and compliance. He ruffled three little blond heads, then his hand skimmed over Laney's darker one and he brushed his fingertips against her cheek. Again, something strong and vital passed between them before he turned away and entered the cockpit.

The return trip was a breeze. The boys were enthralled, and only once when they encountered a bit of turbulence from buffeting winds did Matthew alone seem unnaturally pale and green about the mouth. Laney quickly engaged him in conversation until she had him laughing over some silly joke, the nausea forgotten.

They flew for a while into the western sun, then through its golden light as it dipped behind the Continental Divide. The day had softened to dusk in the lodge valley when they dipped down out of the sky and skipped to a stop on the jewel-blue lake. Encouraged by Laney, the boys applauded an uneventful trip and smooth landing as Danzer brought the craft to the pier. Lil and Hi were waiting there with an eager Kevin and uncertain Annie to engulf the boys with a hearty welcome as they alighted. Laney's parents questioned her about the trip, and she gave them smiling reassurances in answer, omitting by design the aerial acrobatics. Danzer was the last out, and by then the welcoming committee was already leaving. Lillian called a hello, and Hi gave him a thumbs-up sign, both of which he answered with a wave and a smile. He caught Laney by the arm as she started away, his eyes switching back to the receding herd of children and their enthusiastic shepherds until they were quite out of earshot.

"You were great up there," he said, turning his full attention to her. He did not, she noted, release his hold on her.

"Thanks," she said. "I enjoyed it."

"I could tell. You're a regular daredevil, aren't you? A little risk seems to give you a real charge."

"No more than you," she said, leveling her gaze, and his thumb spread a tingling sensation over the inside of her elbow. She looked down at it, wondering how so simple a movement could produce such a wealth of feeling.

"I guess it's something else we have in common," he said, and she looked up, puzzled to find his gaze following the progress of her parents and the children.

"What does that mean, 'something else'?" she asked, her old wariness of him beginning to return.

For a long moment he said nothing, and when she followed his line of sight, it was to see the last of the children disappear around the corner of the house, her father immediately behind them. She switched her gaze, knowing now that Dan had waited for this, that he wanted her alone. His dark eyes captured hers, and her defenses went immediately on alert.

"You know," he told her softly. "You know very well." She opened her mouth to deny it, but the words caught with her breath in her throat as he pulled her to him. "You feel it, too," he said, and his free hand went to her face, his thumb bracing her chin and tilting it upward. Electricity surged through her, sharp and hot, and suddenly she was in his arms, his mouth coming down over hers. She was unprepared, swamped by the searing pressure. She felt her defenses crumble, felt her strength to resist dissolve. Her eyelids blinked and closed, and she melted against him, her breasts flattening against the warm wall of his chest. He rotated his head, slowly grinding his mouth against hers, and his hand dropped down to cup her hips, pressing her full-length against him. The tip of his tongue rimmed her teeth, and she waited for one breathless moment for it to slip inside and fill her mouth, unaware that her own tongue rippled in expectation, teasing his, while her arms hung limply at her sides, stunned into uselessness. He did not accept the mindless invitation. Instead, he slowly pulled away, holding her closely still, while her eyelids fluttered open and the strength returned to her knees.

Then, very deliberately, his hands holding her face, his breath tickling her cheek, he kissed her again. This time her arms moved about his waist as his tongue delved into the sweet, dark cavern of her mouth. Her knees went weak again, and she brought her hands up and over the tops of his shoulders, hanging on as her body clamored with needs she hadn't known she possessed. At last, he put her away, slowly, reluctantly. His hands fell from her face, brushing with his knuckles the taut peaks of her breasts in their descent. She trembled, fresh air rushing into her lungs as a measure of sanity returned.

He stared at her, his eyes studying hers, gauging her reaction. He had proved a point; they both knew it, and suddenly fear rose up in her. It was happening. Already the change had begun. He was changing her, changing everything, and all at once she couldn't bear it.

"I won't let you," she said, not knowing herself exactly what she meant. He lifted a hand entreatingly, but she backed away, shaking her head. Regret was on his face, and that, too, was somehow unacceptable. She whirled away.

"Laney, I shouldn't have. I, I couldn't help myself."

But she was beyond hearing, hurrying now toward the end of the pier and the shore. What was happening to her? She was strong, yet had lost control of her own body for a short while. She didn't like the idea that this could happen, didn't like that he had made it happen so easily. But could she, would she, stop it from happening again? That was the question she had to ask herself.

Chapter Four

He tried to talk to her. More than once he made an opportunity to be alone with her. He tagged along when she took the kids into the woods and then dreamed up excuses to send them off on their own. If she went out to work in the small vegetable garden, he slipped out to "help." If she went to make beds upstairs, he'd become certain she hadn't taken enough linens and insist on saving Lillian the trouble of carrying them up to her. But in every instance, the moment he went beyond the most banal of pleasantries, she bolted like a frightened fawn. After a couple of days of it, he told himself it was just as well. He didn't know what he'd say to her anyway.

The truth was, he didn't really know what had happened that day. The kiss had seemed like such a good idea at the time, and there had been a few moments when he'd thought she was of the same opinion. Then, somehow, it had all changed. One moment she was in his arms, warm, willing and wonderful, and the next she was looking at him like he'd threatened her, frightened her, and he'd known he'd made a mistake. If only he knew with a certainty what that mistake was. He thought he might have rushed her, but the afternoon had been such fun, so easy and interesting and oddly arousing. He'd felt sure it had been that way for her, too, and a kiss had seemed a reasonable, logical, perfectly enjoyable ending to the day.

In the days prior to the flight, he'd indulged himself in a bit of reverse psychology. He'd meant to make her change her mind about him. For some reason it was important that she like him, and he'd decided the way to accomplish that was to pretend otherwise, to be unaware, uninterested in her. For a while, that tack had seemed to be working. In fact, he'd felt certain she'd known just what he'd gotten up to, for the moment he was ready to respond to her obvious interest, she'd turned the tables on him! He'd made short work of it with that stunt in the air—and in a plane grossly unsuitable for such maneuvers. But it had worked, or at least it had seemed to. He'd complimented her, and she'd seemed pleased. She'd seemed so relaxed afterward and so open with him, her old wariness apparently gone. At lunch, she'd sat across the table from him and allowed him to hold her hand as if it was the most natural thing in the world. Later, she'd presented him to the Pettys unabashedly, unashamedly, her hand in his, and when he'd found himself touching her in small, intimate ways, she'd looked at him with such calmness and such *awareness* that he'd assumed she was feeling the magnetic draw between them. He'd told himself that he hadn't been wrong after all, that she was as attracted to him as he was to her.

Then he'd kissed her, boldly, perhaps even a bit recklessly, and suddenly they were right back where they'd started. It just didn't figure. On the other hand, maybe the answer was all too obvious. She was young, perhaps too young, and hers had been a rather sheltered existence in many ways. Then there was this Crater person, too, someone much more attuned to her world, no doubt, someone more her sort. He couldn't help wondering what the deal was there, how close they were, what they expected from each other, if her parents approved of him, if they'd made love...

It was not a productive pastime, thinking about Laney and if she willingly and happily made love to some half-wild mountain man... They couldn't be a very steady thing, though. In the weeks he'd been here he'd never seen the man or known Laney to go to him, not that she couldn't have managed it without his knowing. Also, her parents had never mentioned him except in passing, and that seemed significant. Maybe. He wanted to ask flat out how serious it was between them, but she simply gave him no opportunity even for idle conversation. He'd begun to wonder if it was a lost cause, then late one evening he stepped out of the shower, one towel wrapped around his waist, another draped over his shoulder, and there she was, toothbrush in hand and wearing a big shirt over mannish, pale yellow cotton pajamas.

She had the cap off the toothpaste, and as she spun away from the sink, a great chalky blob of it fell on the floor. Too stunned to notice, she promptly stepped in it.

"Yuck!" The white paste squished between her bare toes, momentarily diverting her attention. Danzer started to laugh, his strong arms folded across his chest, water droplets plastering the dark hairs to his skin. Laney's eyes zipped upward, sharp, sudden anger in them. "It's not funny!" she exclaimed, standing on one foot. Danzer immediately put a clamp on it, but a stubborn smile twisted his lips.

"Let me help you," he said, stepping forward, but she drew back against the sink counter. "Aw, come on." He held up both hands. "You helped me out with the fish guts, didn't you? Of course, you *gave* them to me in the first place." She glared at him, and he laughed, taking the towel from his shoulder into his hands. "Never mind. Hop up there on the counter."

She raked her eyes over him, color pinking her cheeks. "Just get out, will you?"

"Like this?" He indicated the towel about his waist. "Hardly proper, do you think?"

"Didn't you bring clothes with you?"

"Certainly," he said, tossing away the towel in his hand and opening the door of the second stall to lift his jeans from the hook. "You really ought to speak to your father about hooks on the *outside* of these doors."

"I'll do that," she said through her teeth.

He nodded cheerfully, grinning at her. She was disturbed by being here with him like this, and he found that hopeful. Deliberately he slipped the jeans over first one leg and then the other, then slowly pulled them up under the towel and zipped them. Laney made a studied practice of looking away, but the color slowly heightened in her cheeks to a pulsing red, signaling her awareness.

Danzer removed the towel from around his waist and placed it about his neck, leaving his jeans unbuttoned. He bent and snatched the other towel from the floor, then carried it over to the sink, where he dropped it over the smeared blob of toothpaste. Going down on his haunches beside her, he cleaned the goo from the stone floor, and stood again, depositing the towel in the sink to be rinsed later.

"Your turn," he said, sliding both hands through his wet, tousled hair. "Hop up here and put your foot in the sink." She wouldn't quite meet his gaze, but that pretty chin came out at that stubborn angle.

"Why don't you just leave?" she asked caustically.

"I was here first," he answered. "Why don't you go?"

"I have toothpaste on my foot!"

He tapped her chin with a damp forefinger. "That's why you need to put your foot in the sink." She rolled her eyes, and her mouth opened to protest, but he stopped her with a look of mock sternness and a gentle admonition. "Ah-ah-ah. Turnabout's fair play, now isn't it? Come on." Before she could object, he clamped his hands about her waist and lifted her easily onto the counter between the two sinks. She was lighter than he'd expected, though she was tall for a woman and looked strong and athletic in her jeans and flannels. Her hands came up automatically as he lifted her, falling on his shoulders for steadiness. The contact was exciting, vivid, and just for a moment her pale green eyes met his. She felt it, too, the electricity that passed between them, or he was not the judge he imagined himself.

She pulled her hands back and dropped her gaze. He took advantage of that small display of vulnerability, turning her sideways, one hand on her arm, the other at her ankle. She did not resist, and he placed her foot in the sink, struggling with the urge to run his hand up her leg. He reached for the spigot handles and turned on the water, adjusting the temperature carefully. She said nothing, her hands braced against the side of the sink behind her. He washed her foot, sliding his fingers between her toes and gently rubbing them clean. She flinched a couple of times and gasped once, as if he was hurting or tickling her; he knew it wasn't the former. When he glanced at her, it was to find her bottom lip clamped between her teeth, nostrils flaring and chest heaving with deep, sharp breaths. She was not unaffected. Smiling, he turned off the water and slid the towel from about his neck, draping it over her foot. His fingers massaged away the moisture from ankle to toes.

Finished at last, he tossed away the towel and turned her to face him, his hands at her waist. Gently he lifted her from the countertop and set her on her feet, deliberately holding his place. Her pale eyes grew wide, the tips of her breasts brushing his chest provocatively through the thin cotton as she caught her breath.

"You know, this wouldn't have happened if you'd knocked before barging in," he said evenly.

"I—I thought everyone was asleep."

"Nope."

"W-well, I'll go and let you...do...whatever you were doing."

She attempted to slip away, but he held her in place with his hands at her waist.

"Actually I'm through," he told her, "almost." The water ran from his hair down the back of his neck and between his shoulder blades. A shiver ran down his spine, and she seemed to pick it up. He felt her trembling, and suddenly he desperately needed to kiss her.

He slid his arms around her waist and tightened them, feeling the contact in his groin as their bodies came together. She felt as if she might shake to pieces in his hands and was breathing raggedly through her mouth. She wanted this. He had to believe she wanted this. He was sure of it, doubtless. How could he be mistaken with that pulse throbbing there in the delicate hollow of her throat, with her hands creeping up his arms and that delicious tremor shaking her? He ducked his head and brought his mouth to hers, their lips melding in incredible softness.

It was as if someone put a match to him. White hot and urgent desire swept through him. He let his hands wander up her back, plundering her mouth, delving inside with his tongue. He thought of making love to her, of carrying her upstairs to his room and closing the door, peeling her clothes away and feasting with hands and mouth and eyes on her young, supple body. She would help him, of course, willingly, eagerly, passion sending her hands over his body, clutching him, kneading...

Suddenly he became aware of a steady pressure on his chest, pushing, struggling against his strength. Her mouth tore away from his, her back arching against his arms. Instantly he released her, and she bolted, drawing up short against the door. One look at her face and he knew he'd messed up again. What was it about him that did this to her? Only a moment before he'd been certain that she wanted him, that she felt the same compelling attraction for him that he felt for her. But there was that look again, that frightened, frantic, puzzled, miserable look. He reached out a hand to her.

"Laney, what's . . ."

She whirled and yanked open the door, disappearing behind it. Danzer stared, stunned, confused. It had happened again. He'd done it again, whatever it was. He closed his hands into fists and whacked the counter top. This was crazy. This couldn't be happening to him. Why couldn't she just talk to him, tell him what troubled her about him? He could make her see that he meant her no harm, that they could get along, even enjoy each other. He stepped to the side and turned on the water, rinsing the toothpaste from the towel he'd used to clean the floor. Somehow he had to make her understand that she could relax with him. Tomorrow he would make her sit down with him and discuss this thing.

She wasn't at breakfast, and she wasn't at lunch, and she wasn't anywhere else in the place as far as he could tell. There were six extra mouths to feed, counting his own, but for once Laney was not at her mother's side to help with the cooking and cleaning. She just, simply, wasn't there, and no one but him seemed to notice.

His appetite was not particularly acute that day, and both Lil and Hi commented on that fact; yet, neither so much as mentioned Laney's name. He figured it wasn't any of his business, and he said nothing, but she wasn't there later in the afternoon, either, because he looked around for her. She was not in the garden, and she was not in the house, and she was not feeding the chickens or tending the bony old cow they kept for milk. She was not in the work shed, and she was not in the storage shed. No wood had been chopped that day since he and Hi had added to the stack that morning, and she was on no part of the lake he could see. About five o'clock he told Hi he needed to take the plane up to check out an odd sound he thought he'd detected in the engine. He flew back and forth over that valley, from mountaintop to treetop, and he saw no sign of another human being beyond the lodge site. All he accomplished was the wasteful burning of precious fuel—and making himself feel like a bona fide idiot, a feeling Hi reinforced for him at dinnertime.

It had been hours since anyone, to Danzer's knowledge, had seen her, so it didn't seem suspect or amiss at that point to mention her absence. He tried to appear nonchalant about it. He sliced his patty of venison sausage, laid down his knife, took up his fork, and lifted the bite-size piece almost to his mouth before he seemed to have a thought, looked up unexpectedly and asked in the most casual tone, "Where has Laney gotten off to? It occurs to me I haven't seen her since this morning." He then put the bite of sausage in his mouth and chewed appreciatively.

Hi was buttering a tall, golden biscuit, and he proceeded thoughtfully, his high forehead wrinkling. "I don't know," he said. "She goes off on her own occasionally. She say anything to you, Lil?"

Lillian shook her head. "Not to me. She seemed pretty skittish at breakfast, though. When she gets that way, she sometimes just takes off."

"The girl needs to be away once in a while. Been that way a long time. She's probably gone up to see Crater. She has a need to be with him ever' so often."

Danzer couldn't believe what he was hearing. An otherwise responsible twenty-three-year-old woman just disappears in the middle of a wilderness without a word to anyone, and her otherwise responsible parents just calmly assume she's developed a "need" for some antisocial, nature nut camping out on the mountainside under some pine tree somewhere! He considered himself a broad-minded fellow, and he'd availed himself of the company of a willing woman friend when he'd felt a particular need to do so, and he supposed his own parents during their lifetimes had known he was likely to do that, had even been aware of certain moments when he'd done just that very thing. But never in his wildest dreams had he ever imagined they would sit around the dinner table with a guest and calmly intimate the sort of things Laney's parents had just intimated to him. It was not, a surprisingly pristine new moral code told him, *proper*. It was not *right*. And he, for one, was outraged. Fortunately he was also sensible enough to remember there were children at the table. Little pitchers have big ears and all that.

He got a firm hold on himself, and, quite naturally, he laid aside his fork. Just as naturally he leaned forward on his elbows, put on a calm expression and said, "Don't you think she's had plenty of time to..." Here his composure failed him. He nearly choked on the words. He sat up straight, cleared his throat, took a drink of fresh, sweet water, and tried again. "When, I wonder, do you suppose she'll return?"

Hi shrugged unconcernedly, his attention focused chiefly on his dinner. "If she's not back by tomorrow night, I reckon we ought to go lookin' for her, though I'll warrant there's no need. That girl can take care of herself."

The color drained out of Dan's face. He sent a desperate look at Lillian, who raised her eyebrows over the rim of her glass as if to say, "What? Is there something else you wanted to know?"

Dan pushed his plate away, the few bites he'd taken turning sour in his stomach. He felt ill, quite literally ill. "My stomach's kind of rubbery today," he mumbled, swiveling to throw first one leg then another over the bench he shared with Mark, Matt and Mike. "I think I need some fresh air."

He excused himself, aware of Lillian's worried expression and Hi's curious one but not caring a fig, for once, what they thought. He was disappointed in those two, bitterly disappointed, but then that's what he got for meddling in matters that were clearly none of his business. He went out and walked up and down the pier, feeling small and helpless against the vast, sparkling canvas of the sky. He stared at the black, irregular wall of mountains, and it seemed to him that he was in the pit of a volcano, ringed by dark, brooding, forbidding rock, and a few planks were all that stood between him and a hidden, all-consuming fire. He looked into the black, feathery silence of the forest, and he knew she was in there somewhere. Maybe she was fine, and maybe she was not. One alternative did not seem particularly favorable to another, for if she was fine, she was fine with another man, and if she was not, there wasn't a blasted thing he could do about it.

He was out of his depth here. Had he been foolish enough to strike out on his own looking for her, he knew beyond doubt that he would never find her and that before morning someone else would just have to come looking for him. Slowly, reluctantly, Danzer Wilson came to a hard realization. He had no control in this situation. For once, he had no control. He couldn't woo her. He couldn't ignore her. He couldn't even *find* her. But at least he had the satisfaction of knowing he'd gotten to her. She was attracted to him, she might not like it, but she was.

She's probably gone up to see Crater. She has a need to be with him every so often. Him. She had a need to be with Crater. Had his kisses driven her to him? That wasn't the way it was supposed to be. Nothing was as it was supposed to be. This fantasy was not turning out as he'd imagined. This dream had definitely fizzled, and were he less the man than he was, he'd have climbed in his plane and taken off for more familiar territory, he'd have told the Scotts to forget their little verbal contract, to find themselves another man. But he knew he wouldn't leave before his contract was fulfilled. He knew he'd stay every single day of his three months. And he knew he'd think of Laney up there on that mountainside with some other man who probably fulfilled her needs in ways his ego wouldn't allow him to contemplate. No, this fantasy was not working out as he'd come to envision it, not at all. Not at all.

Laney sat before the fire, her knees drawn up beneath her chin, her arms about her legs. Normally she would not have stared into the flames, for one was blind long seconds afterward, and there were dangers on the mountainside at night, especially when chaperoning an inexperienced party. But she was not doing the chaperoning tonight, and Crater's notch was as familiar and safe to her as her own home. She loved this place. A natural draft pulled the smoke up and out of the cave at the top of the notch far overhead. In the morning, the dawning sun lit the gently curving slit in the rock with a rosy glow. At noonday, it illuminated the room with a brilliant shaft of light. And at all hours the tapering slit, wide at the bottom and narrow at the top, brought fresh, clean air into the cavern buried inside some thirty feet of solid rock. The opening was hidden behind a pair of tall, sturdy pines, and their elegant spires served to filter the smoke that wafted through their spiky needles.

Crater maintained that this natural refuge had sheltered man for untold centuries, and he had found enough evidence to lend a measure of credence to his assertion. He kept these treasures, shaped bits and pieces of wood and stone, in a secret part of the cave where even Laney had never been permitted. He talked of elaborate drawings and paintings deep within the heart of the mountain, but these, too, if they existed, he protected from all other eyes. The "brains" would descend, he insisted, if his discovery were made known. They would dig and probe and gouge until the sacredness of the place was completely destroyed. He had told Laney once that he had been one of the "plunderers" until his sense had overcome his book learning and he had finally understood that the earth was a living being to be respected and protected rather than exploited. Then again, he'd also told her that he was a reincarnation of a powerful Indian warrior of the seventeenth century. Laney believed neither and both.

However odd he might be, Crater was a friend to be trusted, and it was to him that she came when life was most confusing and difficult. He always said it was this place that drew her, a natural shelter created by the earth for those who best knew her, and at moments like this, Laney almost believed him. He fed a stick to the fire and chanted something low and guttural as it burned. Laney sighed, her melancholy permeating even the sanctuary of this place. Crater shook his long, white hair out of his face, then pulled a strip of leather from the pocket of his faded shirt and tied it back, making a ponytail at the nape of his neck almost as long as the beard that hung from his chin and spread over his thin chest.

"This man," he said, taking up their conversation where they'd left off a half-hour before, "what's 'is name, then?"

"Dan," she replied, "Danzer Wilson."

He stroked his beard lovingly. "Sounds Scandinavian. He a big, blond man, you say?"

Laney shook her head. "He's big, tall, real tall, but his hair is dark, very dark, almost black, and his eyes, too." She stared at the fire, seeing dark eyes where yellow flames danced.

Crater watched her, his fingers stroking thoughtfully. "You like 'im?"

"No," she said, then, "Yes. I mean, sometimes I do and sometimes I don't."

"But you trust 'im."

It was not a question, but she felt compelled to answer as if it were. "I don't know." She held her breath a moment, wanting it to sound reasonable, sane. "He frightens me," she finally said. "He frightens me in a way I can't describe. Yet, I know he wouldn't . . . harm me. Or at least I think I know."

She lowered her eyes and chewed her lip, obviously wanting to say more but thinking better of it. Crater cleared his throat, wondering if she had admitted even to herself what feelings this man aroused in her. For a moment, he felt a sudden, primordial rage at this man, and the next he surrendered to the natural order of things, the inevitability of it. She was no little girl any longer, no senseless creature. It was the way of man that innocence must eventually give way to experience and experience to wisdom. It was for this that the Maker gave us urges and instincts, and this child of the mountain had been given a heart of such goodness and instincts so fine that she needed little else to protect her. The years had proved that to him.

In all the countless days and nights he had kept watch over her from a distance, never once had he had to step in, to save her from her own actions or those of another, not that danger had never sought her. He could remember times that still made his heart crawl into his throat and quiver, but in every instance she had been aware, had done the things that brought her safely away, until one day he had made himself stay at home and abandon his secret shadowings of her. He could laugh over that now. Like all men, he suffered from an inflated sense of superiority. He had believed that he was one with the mountain, that his skills were so above those of all others that he could not be found out. Then she had come to him, a child still, her brow furrowed, her eyes worried.

"I thought you might be sick," she had said. "Where have you been? I looked for you, but you weren't there. Dad said I'd imagined you, that you hadn't been there all along, but I know. It was our game, our way."

The shock had nearly cracked his gruff facade. He was proud still that he had managed to act unmoved, to hold back his tears, to mutter and complain and hold her at the proper distance. At last she had understood. She didn't need him anymore. He trusted her to care for herself. She had put her strong, young arms about his neck and wept into his beard until, grumbling, he had sent her away and told her not to come back. She hadn't obeyed him, of course, and he had discovered that he was still needed—only in another way. She came to him when she had need of confidence and safety and clarification. She shared her weaknesses with him, and he knew it was a singular compliment, an act of total trust. He suspected they had been father and daughter in another life and that he had not done so well by her then, but this he kept to himself out of fear that she would tarnish her image of him—and that it might not have been as he dreamed it had, after all, that his obsession to know her, to care for her had been nothing more than an old man's loneliness for the things of life he had rejected.

He fed another stick to the fire and made his little chant.

"You like him," he said, "but he troubles you. In some ways you trust him, in others you don't."

She nodded and sighed and laid back upon the powdered sand, her shins a wall between her and the fire. "He kissed me," she said out of the darkness behind her knees. "He kissed me, and I was scared. I liked it, but I was scared."

He nodded his understanding, his strongest suspicions confirmed, and something in him closed and folded up. "Your pa like 'im?" he heard himself ask, not that it mattered, really, except to him. Somehow, he needed to know.

"Yes," she answered him, "Mom, too."

Crater wrote in the dirt with his finger. Finally he stopped, looked at what he had written, and wiped it out.

"Well, you'll make out okay," he said, getting stiffly to his feet. "I'm sure of that." He wiped his hands on his pant leg and walked to the bed. He pulled a ragged army blanket from the untidy tangle on his narrow cot and tossed it to her. She moved away from the fire and stretched out on her side, spreading the cover over her body. He sat on the edge of the bed and removed the boots from his bare feet, but she didn't bother, curling up boots and all on the sandy floor.

He laid back, fully clothed, and stuck his feet beneath the blankets jumbled on his bed. For long minutes, both of them were quiet. Only the fire spoke into the silence, but something must have told her he was not asleep.

"How do you know?" she asked finally. It was a ritual question, one she'd asked so many times about so many things that it had become a special signal between them, a sign of respect and caring. Often he'd had facts to give her, secrets to tell, scientific and proved. Other times, he had only emotion to offer, feelings real and imagined. Tonight he had both.

"Because," he said, "you have the best instincts of any female I've ever known." He ground his few teeth together, wishing he'd said "woman."

"Then you think I should just follow my instincts where Dan's concerned?" she pressed timidly, sounding more like a little girl than she had in a long time.

"I think," he said, rolling onto his side, his face to the wall, "that you don't have much choice. No need to worry about it, though. You're sound in head and heart. You just follow their lead and you'll wind up where you need to go." There, he'd said it. He heard her rise up on her elbow, knew she was watching his back. What was she thinking? She told him, as if she'd heard the unspoken question.

"Crater," she said pleadingly, "you'll always be here, won't you?"

Tears sprang to his eyes, and this time he let them fall. "Where the hell else would I go?" he snapped, his voice even more gravelly than usual.

"That's what I mean," she rejoined quickly. "You wouldn't ever go back to the world, would you?"

He wiped his nose and answered her. "This is my world. There ain't no other."

She was quiet for a moment, and he heard her lie back down, her head on her hands, as was so often the case. "I'm glad," she said. "I couldn't bear it if you were to leave here. I can't think of this place without you, at least."

He didn't know what that meant, and he couldn't ask, not without compromising. Instead he said, "I'll be here. I'll die here. Now go to sleep. Your blabbin's keepin' me awake."

He lay for a long while, listening as she slipped into sleep, her breath a soft whisper in the background of his thoughts. His tears dried. His resolve returned. She had never been his little girl, except perhaps in another life or in the fanciful dreams of an old man. What did it matter anyway? Little girls grow up. It was the way of all life. If this man was not the one, there would be another, now that the time had truly come. She would not make a mistake, he was confident of that, and so he was content, much, he suspected, as her parents were content, with full hearts and gladness and tears and sadness. Life was ever thus, would ever be so, and he wouldn't change his, couldn't, not now, nor interfere with hers. She had her own life to live, her own destiny to fulfill, and he liked to think he had been a part of it, an important part.

"Where have you been? I looked for you, but you weren't there.... It was our game, our way."

He closed his eyes and slept, dreaming of a tall man with dark hair and eyes, not the man she dreamed of, but a man he had dreamed of before, a man in skins and feathers and braids, a man at one with his world, a man who haunted him, possessed him—the man he would be, had he a choice, the man he had tried to be before he'd understood that we cannot always choose. Sometimes a person can only play the role destiny assigns, and all that matters is that he—or she—plays it well.

Laney came down through the woods humming. She had a catch in her back and a kink in her neck, but she didn't care. Sleeping on the ground was never easy, not even when the ground was powdery soft and familiar, yet she liked it. The world felt right today, and that was all that mattered. She had awakened to find Crater gone and knew that he wished for no goodbye, so she'd simply slipped through the notch and started home, unaccountably happy with the morning.

She saw him long before she drew near enough to acknowledge his presence, his back against a large stone through which a tree had grown up at a slant. He stood away from it and turned to face her as soon as the sounds of her careless walk made her known to him, and she smiled, thinking how long he had been unaware while she had watched and drawn nearer. He was the innocent here, the uninitiated. It made her feel in control, mature.

"I was worried about you," he said when she came to a stop before him. She shielded her eyes from the morning brightness, looking up at him.

"Were you? No need to be."

"I see that now."

She started to walk, and he fell in beside her.

"How did you know I'd come this way?" she asked, pleased that his gait was smooth and easy. So many times they couldn't keep up, these greenhorns. He stared ahead into the eastern sun.

"I asked your father."

She cut him a look. "He told you I'd be with Crater then."

He nodded, his gaze studious. "I didn't like it much."

She stopped, and he stopped a pace later, turning to look at her. "Why not?"

He gaped, looked away, laughed mirthlessly, looked again. "Why do you think?"

"I can't imagine," she told him, and he stared, as if not quite believing her.

"Look," he began, pausing to swallow, "when a man likes a woman, when he *thinks* about a woman, he doesn't want to think about..." He paused again, then plunged ahead. "He doesn't want to think about her being with another man."

She cocked her head to one side, wondering if he actually meant what she thought he meant and deciding that, somehow, he did. A smile teased her mouth. "You're jealous."

He looked pained. "Not jealous, exactly, just...not liking it."

She laughed this time, ridiculously pleased. She knew he was attracted to her, but enough to be jealous? Was this genuine or simply male ego? She wasn't sure, but she wanted to be. She could admit that much now. She mulled over letting him think Crater was something other than a very special friend but decided against it. Dishonesty never helped anything.

"Danzer," she said, "Crater is maybe eighty years old."

He stood quite still for a long moment. "Eighty?"

"Well, maybe seventy," she answered lightly. "He won't tell for sure, but I'd say seventy at least, eighty on the outside. Call it seventy-five."

He blew out a stream of air. "Lord, what an idiot! Holy cow, Laney, I thought he was your boyfriend! I thought he was your..."

"Lover?" she provided. He gave an embarrassed nod. Awkwardness overtook them. She cleared her throat. "Crater's my friend, my teacher, sort of a grandfather figure."

Danzer shrugged, his gaze not quite meeting her eyes. "A grandfather. Well, that explains a lot."

She took a deep breath, needing to keep talking. "I think he might have been an archaeologist," she said chattily, "but that's just a guess because he never talks much about himself. Anyway, it must have been a long time ago, because he was here in these mountains probably before I was even born. He came down one day when it was just Mama and me. I was about three, and I remember Mama was afraid of him at first, but he just wanted to talk to me. That's all he ever wanted, just to be around me for a little while, to tell me things, teach me things." She looked back up into the tall green trees as if she expected him to appear. "He used to be there all the time, watching over me wherever I went, sort of a guardian angel, but I guess he figures I can take care of myself now."

"I guess you can at that," Danzer said softly, and she turned back to him, aware suddenly that he had stepped closer, so close he had but to lift his arms to take her in them. She looked up into his eyes, so dark and so brown and so shiny that she could see herself in them. She smiled at her reflection.

"I want to kiss you," he whispered, and her heartbeat picked up, thrumming so loudly in her ears she wondered that he didn't hear it. "Will you let me kiss you?"

She knew what he was doing. He was asking, because before he had not asked. She put her hand to his face, ran her thumb across his mouth, wanting it, yet uncertain. He wanted more than a kiss, she felt certain, but was she ready for that? She dropped her hand.

"I don't think this is the time." She couldn't tell him anything else, didn't even understand herself, really.

"All right," he said, his voice like the wind in the treetops, but just for a moment he stood there, and she knew if he touched her she would change her mind. She half hoped he would, half needed him to, but at last he stepped away, and the tension seemed to drain out of him. "I'll walk you home," he said; then, laughing, "On the other hand, maybe you'd better walk me home. I need street signs to get where I want to go."

"You could learn," she said, putting her hand in his. He threaded his fingers through hers and grinned lazily.

"If you'd teach me."

She smiled at him and stepped off at a brisk clip. "Another time. Right now I'm hungry!"

"Didn't your grandfather feed you?" he teased, falling in step. She made a face.

"He doesn't keep the best-stocked larder or cook like Mama, for that matter."

"No one cooks like your mother," he declared. "If it wasn't for the wood chopping, I'd get fat."

"Well, now we can't have that," she said most solemnly, picking up the pace. "You couldn't keep up then."

"I can keep up," he assured her, jogging easily at her side.

"I believe you can," she told him, breaking into a run. He laughed and ran after her, catching her hand again as he passed her up, towing her along in his wake, only to have her pull free and dart off in another direction, keeping them on course. When they broke the tree line and started into the clearing that held the lodge, they were walking side by side, breathless with laughter and exertion and conversation. It struck Laney that things had somehow changed. Already, so much had changed. Was that good or was that bad? She didn't know anymore. She just didn't know.

Chapter Five

"More coffee, Dan?"

"Why, yes. Thank you, Laney."

"You're very welcome."

"You're very kind."

"You're both very nauseating," Hi grumbled, pushing his own cup across the table for his daughter to refill. "I think," he said, drawing it back full, "I liked you better when you couldn't abide each other."

"They never did any such thing," Lillian protested good-naturedly from the sink, but the pair in question traded loaded glances.

"Wonderful breakfast, Lil," Danzer said, changing the subject.

"Thank you, dear. I always say nothing starts the day like a good meal."

"Absolutely," Danzer agreed, and Laney felt compelled to put in her two cents worth.

"You're so right, Mama."

Hi rolled his eyes. "I'm getting a bellyache. All this sweetness and light is more than I can stomach." He pushed his chair back and stomped out, muttering a string of words that made Lillian snap her dish towel at him.

"Never mind him," she counseled patiently. "He's feeling kind of closed in. Always happens this time of year. Personally I think we ought to just pack up and strike out for a few days, kids 'n' all."

Laney looked at Danzer. It was a habit she'd acquired rather quickly over these past few days, checking his reaction. He, on the other hand, had acquired the habit of reacting for her, and he did so now, tilting his head with one brow cocked at an interesting angle. She smiled at him, and his hand lightly skimmed the side of her thigh on its way from his lap to the table. A shock of electricity passed through her, leaving a warm, fluid tightness in its wake. It always happened the same way. A bump on the landing, a brush on the stairway, a bit of playful tussling on the dock, and this feeling jolted through her, hot and compelling and liquid. Her breath would catch in her throat, and her heart would speed erratically, and for a moment she could think of nothing and no one but him.

It happened now. She drew a blank for several seconds, her gaze fastened on his hand, the memory of the sensation it had caused when it brushed her thigh still coursing through her like the echo of a wild, erotic call rolling back at her from the mountaintop. She felt a tightness in her chest and instinctively pulled a deep breath, jump-starting her thoughts along the path they had abandoned moments before. She cleared her throat.

"I think that's a wonderful idea, Mama. We'd all enjoy a few nights on the mountain. It'd be good for Dad, the kids love it, and Dan's never been."

"We'll do it then," Lillian said over her shoulder. "Why don't you go out and put it to him, Dan, while Laney and I

finish up these dishes? Goodness, do we have enough
sleeping bags for all these kids? Dan, tell Hi we're going to
need that extra pack he's been meaning to repair.''

''I'll take care of it,'' he said, rising from his chair. Dan
rested his hand on Laney's shoulder, and she smiled up at
him dreamily. He winked and grazed her jawline with his
knuckles as he left her. Laney surfaced from the swamp of
sensation that seemed to always follow his touch to find her
mother staring at her, a knowing little smile on her lips. The
color flamed in Laney's face. She snatched her cup and
gulped coffee.

''He likes you,'' Lillian commented idly, ''and I'd say you
like him.''

Laney gasped and choked, spluttering coffee. ''Wh-
who?''

Lillian gave her a narrow look that clearly communi-
cated her acuity. ''Just clear the table,'' she said, turning
back to her sink. ''And think it through, Laney. He's not
like us. You need to be sure what you're letting yourself in
for. Remember that.''

Laney left the dishes on the table and went quickly to put
her arms around her mother's shoulders. ''I promise,'' she
whispered, and Lillian pressed her arm with her cheek, her
hands in dishwater up to her elbows. Lillian straightened
and smiled, her eyes bright and full.

''You're right, you know,'' she said softly. ''Everything
is changing. But that's not so bad, is it? We grow older, and
life changes. That's the way of it, but it is a little sad. Not
that I don't want you to have what I've had, a husband, a
child. It just seems that it was yesterday when you were three
and Crater came crawling down off that mountain, so big
and hairy and tattered. I'll never forget the look on his face,
the way he knelt at your feet and how you thumped his
cheek with your little hand. I sensed the change coming
then, and sure enough, before I knew it you were running

around these woods like a wild Indian. In some ways it seemed Crater had more of you than Dad and I. But it was all right, because you were so happy, and it'll be all right as long as you stay that way. That's what I wanted to tell you. That's what Dad wants you to understand, too.''

Laney tightened her hug. "I'll be happy, Mama. I don't know how to be anything else. You and Dad have always seen to that."

Lillian smiled and sniffed and patted her daughter's forearm with a wet hand. "You're going to make me cry. Stop it now and clear the table, you hear? There's five kids to be outfitted for camping, and here I am bawling into my dishwater. Do something useful, why don't you?''

Laney laughed and said, "I'll take care of the kids. You just wash these." She quickly gathered the dishes and left them on the wooden countertop, giving her mother one more quick hug before hurrying out.

The children marched through the woods like little soldiers, with Hi and Lillian breaking trail and Laney and Dan bringing up the rear. Each of the children carried a small pack and each of the adults a large one. Hi wore a pair of binoculars around his neck on a strap and a nylon rope looped over one shoulder. Lil used a sturdy walking staff honed from a tree branch and polished smooth except for the many irregular knots left on several inches of each end, while Dan and Laney took turns pulling a light, aluminum travois loaded with provisions tied beneath a folded tarp. Everyone carried extra clothing and gloves, and each wore a long-sleeved shirt over jeans, a billed hat and sturdy shoes.

The kids sang for a while, but the going soon got rough enough to require their full attention. They hiked straight up the slope through the trees for a good bit, then small rocks began to crop out in odd places, potential trip-ups for the unwary. Small rocks gave way to large ones, and trees grew scarcer. They sat beside a stream and ate a cold lunch, making a picnic out of it and allowing the children to rest, but all were eager to continue, and they soon found themselves on the trail again. By mid-afternoon they began to encounter ledges and slides too wide to go around, and they slowly picked their way through and over them, climbing rather than hiking. Lillian's staff came in handy then. Grasping one knotted end and offering the other, she could give the smallest children a needed tug up slopes too steep for their little legs to manage.

They were headed for a place called Cathedral Pines where two huge slabs of stone had piled up against one another to form a peaked arch. Dirt had showered down on top of them, and over the years trees had taken root and grown up, so that the effect was essentially that of an open cathedral in the side of the mountain with pines on the roof. Lillian was particularly taken with the place, but Hi liked it, too. It seemed to hold a special significance for them that they had never shared with anyone else. Getting to it was not terribly difficult as it was far from the mountain's snowy pinnacle, but the shortest route was up the face of a sheer cliff about a hundred feet high, and that did not seem wise with five children in tow. The alternate route, however, was much longer, and they stopped to rest twice more before facing their final obstacle.

It was not the daunting climb they would have faced had they taken the more direct route, but to Danzer it would have seemed sheer folly to take six (including himself) inexperienced climbers up that steep, rocky escarpment. Laney saw that feeling of doubt on his face, and she found a moment during the preparations for the climb to step close in front of him and flatten her hand against the small valley in the center of his broad chest.

"Trust me," she whispered, and a look of shock flitted across his face.

"Am I that transparent?" he asked softly, and she answered with an apologetic smile. "Or is it just that you already know me too well?"

She felt his hand, heavy and warm, against the small of her back beneath her pack, and as usual the impact rocked her. She gazed up at him, the smile on her lips slackening to an expression of expectation.

"I don't know you nearly as well as I want to," she said, and his head dipped slightly toward hers, his mouth hovering just within reach. She felt the urge to go up on tiptoe and bring her mouth against his, but just when she thought she must, his eyes lifted from hers and a sharp awareness descended. She turned quickly, answering too abruptly perhaps the small voices around her. She was keenly conscious of him as he moved smoothly to aid in the pulling on of gloves and the tightening of shoelaces and the lifting off of packs. More than once their shoulders collided and their hands met over the same small piece of wool or length of string or nylon strap. Then there was another moment just before Hi began the initial ascent when their eyes met, and it was even more physical than a touch. He drew a deep breath and looked away, but an instant later he looked back, and she felt his bare hand clasp hers. She curled her fingers about his, and somehow that connection was satisfying enough to allow her to turn her attention to her father as he climbed.

It was a quick ascent, as she knew it would be, and Hi left spikes at convenient intervals for those who followed. It was Laney's job to remove them as she came up last. Once over the top, Hi secured the rope and tossed one end of it down. Laney dropped Danzer's hand and caught it. As she quickly fashioned a sling, his hand settled on her back and stayed there. When she stooped to slip the rope in place around Kevin's upper body, Danzer transferred his hand to the top of her shoulder, and when she stood again, his arm slipped naturally about her waist.

Lillian went up with Annie, and then the Petty boys followed in order, youngest first. When Danzer's turn came, he paused to look uncertainly at the small mountain of packs and the travois waiting to be hauled up.

"I know the answer to this," he said, "but I have to ask it anyway. You sure you can handle that alone?" He pointed to the mound of packs. She rolled her eyes and struck a cryptic pose, hands on hips.

"If you know the answer, why do you have to ask?"

"Male pride," he admitted drolly. "I wouldn't know where to begin."

"Well, I do. Besides, Dad needs you up top to help him pull, so quit stalling."

He made a face and shook his head, then stepped into the loop of the sling. "I'm going, I'm going. Just forget I said anything, okay, hon?"

"Okay, *hon*," she answered back, helping him pull the loop up over his hips. He caught her hands, stilling them about his waist.

"That was not condescension."

"I didn't think it was."

His thumbs made circles on the insides of her wrists.

"You're beautiful," he whispered. "Did you know that?"

Suddenly her heart was pounding like a jackhammer. She turned her hands in his and clasped both tightly. "I'm glad you think so."

Again his mouth descended toward hers. Their lips brushed, and Laney stepped closer. His hands slid up her arms, and she tilted her head, anticipating what would come next. Just then a small shower of rocks and dirt rained down on them, and Laney jerked back. Hi stood on the very precipice of the cliff, grinning. He cupped his hands around his mouth.

"You two gonna make camp down there, or you comin' up?"

Dan shot Laney a disappointed look. "Don't forget where we left off," he said, then he turned to the rock face and called loudly that he was ready to climb.

Laney stood back, her hands clasped behind her back. He thought she was beautiful! And because he thought she was beautiful, she felt beautiful. The way he looked at her sometimes, the way he touched her, even by accident, said more than any words could. Still, she found she treasured the words, and that surprised her, for words had so often seemed unnecessary in the past.

She watched him climb, taking an odd pleasure in the way he handled himself. He was careful enough to let her know that he did not take this lightly, but his movements were sure and agile as he found his holds and the spikes. The muscles bulged in his upper arms, legs and hips, straining the sleeves of his plaid shirt and the denim of his jeans. Once, he looked down at her and smiled, and she waved, seeing that he enjoyed himself. He waved back and went on, rolling over the top seconds later. She watched him disappear and waited for the rope. After a moment, he walked to the edge, the rope looped about his arm. He gave the end a whirl and let it go. It sailed through the air and landed precisely at her feet. She looked up at him and made a showy bow, which he acknowledged with a salute.

Working quickly, she passed the rope through the pack straps and the curved travois handle and tied it tightly. Next, she checked the travois to be certain everything was properly secured. Finally she waved a signal, and again he answered with a salute before disappearing behind the rim. The rope became taut and the bundle slowly began to move.

When it was a quarter of the way up, Laney started her own climb. As she went, she removed the spikes, slipping them into a small canvas bag tied about her waist. She dropped one but made note of where it landed so that they might retrieve it on their way back, then went on. She climbed bare-handed, as she preferred to do, without the added safety of the lead rope. The gravelly feel of the rock was as familiar to her as that of her own doorknob, and she enjoyed the physical stress of hauling and pushing one's way up the ragged face of the escarpment. The climb took perhaps fifteen minutes. She wasn't even breathing heavily until she went over the edge into Danzer's arms.

He hauled her to her feet, his arms going around her protectively, and half walked, half dragged her away from the edge. She was enjoying the closeness too much to notice he was angry. His hand had found a place under her arm, his fingers pressing against the fullness of her breast, and even through the thickness of her bra, shirt and vest she felt branded, claimed. Then suddenly he was shaking her, his fingers biting into the flesh of her upper arms.

"Don't ever do that again." His voice was not loud but stern, commanding. "What did you think you were doing, climbing without the rope? What kind of an example do you want to set for these children? Would you want to see one of *them* climbing without any safety precautions whatsoever?"

She was too stunned to say or do anything in her own defense. She just stared up at him, open-mouthed and a little hurt. He released her and strode away, his movements stiff and heavy, snatching up his pack as he went after Lillian and the kids. An assortment of feelings barraged her: confusion, surprise, embarrassment, anger and, finally, a kind of awe.

Hi walked up, her pack in hand, and thrust it at her. "I tried to tell him," he said.

"What?"

"That talkin' to you is like talkin' to the wind sometimes, but it seems he doesn't listen, either."

She stared at him, still not comprehending, and he
laughed, scratching his head.

"Haven't I always told you to use the rope?" he said.

"Yes, but I..."

"Never do," he finished for her. "Well, I told him that,
and he said, 'She, by God, will from now on or she's not
climbing again.'"

Laney's eyes opened wide, and she snatched the pack out
of his hand. "Who does he think he is? He can't keep me
from climbing!"

Hi just grinned. "I don't know, Laney," he said, slipping his hand into his pocket and nodding at Danzer's re-
treating back. "He looks to me like the fellow who just
might be able to get it done."

He stepped off after the others, hurrying to overtake the
point. Laney stared after him, letting his words sink in.
Gradually her features softened, and a small smile played
across her lips. Dan cared. He hadn't liked her climbing
without a rope, and that had to mean he cared. But he
wouldn't stop her from climbing, she decided, and that was
final. Still, he evidently cared enough to try, and that meant
something, something important. She swung the pack up
and struggled into it, shaking her head at what had happened, and she realized then how very much she wanted him
to care. She hung her thumbs in the pack straps and started
off, with a great deal, suddenly, to occupy her mind, as she
made her way.

Pensive and preoccupied, she stayed behind for the remainder of the trip, not even spelling Danzer with the travois. She knew quite well that he could manage without her
help, just as he must have known she could manage without his. It had seemed important in the beginning to share

the responsibility, to prove that she was at least as capable as he was. Usually she left no doubt in any man's mind that, in her milieu, her skills and her judgment were superior, and he could darn well follow her lead or he could stay behind, period. But this was different, or she'd thought it was. Now she wondered.

She was torn between being her usual assertive, stubborn self and being meekly submissive. What was right? she wondered. She was glad he cared, and she wanted him to continue caring; but she needed him to understand that she was capable and trustworthy in ways other women often were not. Only once before had she ever attempted to alter her behavior, to be something she was normally not, and she had fond memories of that weekend in Seattle. *He* had had dark hair and dark eyes, too, and she had been pleased by his attentions even though she knew nothing could ever come of them. That had been a single weekend out of her life, and she had known all along that it would never be more. Still, it had been great fun to be courted and squired about and flirted with. She would always remember that young man fondly, but it was different with Dan somehow. She couldn't quite put her finger on what it was; yet she knew that it was different. She thought of that as they trudged along, but somewhere along the line it ceased to matter. All that mattered was that she wasn't ready to relegate this episode to the heading of a treasured summer.

They made camp about six, and there was a general scramble to get set up before darkness descended. The sky was clear and bright, with clouds banked low in the east and moving away from them—a good sign. They decided to camp in the open under the stars, choosing a spot on the edge of the sizable clearing before the formation called Cathedral Pines. Hi put the two youngest boys to work gathering rocks for a firebreak, while he cleared a level place for it in the center of the campsite. Lil got her "kitchen" in order, using the travois, two large stones and the tarp as pantry and counter. Laney, Kevin and Mark went off with plastic, collapsible jugs for water from the creek running parallel to the campsite some fifty or so yards to the north. Danzer and Annie laid out the bedrolls around the campfire. Annie displayed a penchant for organization and orderliness by pacing off with her little feet exact spaces of about a yard between each sleeping bag. Dan did his part by policing the area for rocks and sticks that might interfere with tolerable sleeping and by placing the bedrolls where young Annie solemnly directed.

By the time Laney and the boys returned with the water, Hi was ready to build a fire. He and the kids went in search of enough kindling to get an adequate cooking fire going. Dan moved to Lil's side, expecting that Laney would join them and hoping for a moment when he could communicate with a look or a gesture that he had thought better of his earlier admonition.

He didn't know why he'd done what he'd done. His initial response to the climb had been based upon the fact that there were children along. It had just seemed like a lot to ask a kid to do, but then he'd seen how adaptable kids could be and how trusting and brave. He'd felt proud of every one of them, and any remaining uneasiness had to do strictly with not making a fool of himself. He'd never attempted mountain climbing before, and while he didn't doubt that he could do it, he was also keenly aware of the fact that Laney was probably an expert. He didn't want to look like a buffoon or a coward in front of her, and he knew she'd sensed his misgivings from the very beginning.

He'd enjoyed the climb. He liked physical activity. But it had been more difficult than he'd imagined. It was, in fact, hard work requiring adequate strength, and the potential for disaster seemed to make every possible precaution a necessity. He'd been watching from above when

Laney had signaled to pull up the gear, and he'd helped with that as expected. He'd even hurried to free the rope so he could feed it back down to her. Then, when he'd gone to the edge to do just that, his heart had stopped. She was already halfway up. He'd been dismayed, and it hadn't helped to hear that she made a habit of taking chances like that. All he could think was that she might fall.

It wasn't enough to say simply that he'd overreacted. There was more to it. He'd also overstepped. Laney wasn't a child to be ordered around. She was, in fact, a competent adult, a bit young perhaps but competent and adult, nevertheless. And he hadn't stopped thinking about her for days.

He felt a great sense of relief coupled with hopeful expectation when Laney wandered over to offer her help to her mother. She brought out several cans from the travois, and he was quick to produce the opener. She seemed uncertain what her response should be at first, then slowly a smile turned up the corners of her mouth. His heart did a flip-flop, and it was all he could do not to pull her against him and fold her in a hug. He was still fighting that impulse when Hiram and the boys arrived, their arms full of sticks and dry logs.

"Laney, there's a deadfall around there back of Cathedral Pines. Take the ax and see if you can't get a sizable piece of it free. If you can drag it in whole, we can break it up here and have enough to last us through breakfast tomorrow in one trip."

Instantly she abandoned the cans, took up the small, red-handled ax and walked off. Dan thought immediately of three or four plausible excuses why he should also leave camp, but in the end he simply got up and followed. No one said a word. A couple of the kids watched as if they wanted to come along, but they didn't ask, and he didn't invite them.

They were well away from camp when she stopped and turned. An unfamiliar awkwardness enveloped him. Suddenly he didn't know what to say. She saved him the effort.

"I hope you aren't still angry with me," she said softly, "because if you are, we're going to fight, and I'd really rather not."

A kind of elation whipped through him, and he didn't know quite what to make of it. He looked at her, and oh, heaven, but she was beautiful! Her rich brown hair was pulled back in a thick ponytail that swung at the nape of her neck, and wispy tendrils had escaped to curl softly about her face. In the golden light, her complexion was flawless, clear and glowing with good health; and her eyes shone sea green, a jewellike brightness about them. Oddly her masculine clothing seemed to call attention to her femininity. Her jeans were snug and conformed nicely to her womanly curves, and her breasts were full and firm beneath the shapeless shirt. She wore a narrow belt at her waist, its circumference surprisingly small. Her limbs were long and slender, her shoulders just wide enough to fit comfortably in the curve of his arm, and he knew well that when he took her in his arms, the top of her head came just above his chin. He had a sudden need to do that now. He stepped forward, and when he did, she tossed the ax away and came to meet him.

"I had no right," he said, taking her in his arms. She bowed her head against his shoulder, her palms lying gently against his chest.

"I wasn't showing off," she told him. "I just didn't think."

He meant to make a full explanation, to say that it didn't matter, to tell how frightened he'd been for her but how he understood because he realized now that she really did know what she was doing. But somehow, when he took her face in his hands and tilted it up to his, the words went right out of his head. He couldn't think of anything but how she felt against him. He couldn't see anything but her mouth, full and rosy and softly smiling. He pushed his fingers into her hair and felt the growing tightness in his groin, the desire that throbbed in perfect rhythm with his heart, quickening and strengthening with every beat. He bent his head to hers and felt her mouth soften and mold itself to his.

To his delight, her arms slipped up and around his neck, and he thought, *Oh, yes. Now is the time. Let this be the time.* As if in answer, her hands traveled in different directions, one slipping up his neck and into his hair, the other sliding downward over his shoulder to the center of his back, where it spread flat, holding him to her. He dropped his arms about her, letting his hands move down to the fullness of her hips, and pressed her against him until there could be no doubt in her about how she affected him. He was blatant about it, purposefully so, for he wanted her to understand what he wanted from her, what he would press for if she allowed him to, and yet, he was not prepared for her reaction.

She arched against him, opening her mouth for his tongue and taking it deeply inside her, her own curling beneath it, her hand firm at the back of his head, driving him into her. Shaken, he folded his arms about the small of her back, and she stunned him with the way she clung to him, her body mated to his, as if she meant to leave her imprint along the entire length of him. Her breasts flattened against his chest, firm and supple, and even through the thicknesses of their clothing he felt the pebbly thrust of her nipples. He had a sudden, ungovernable desire to suck them into his mouth and caress them with his tongue.

Automatically his hands went to her hair, catching long, thick swatches of it, while his mouth traveled down her chin and under it, to the smooth column of her throat. He raked his mouth down the side of her throat, the edges of his teeth and the wet tip of his tongue contacting smooth, cool, sensitive skin. She caught her breath and sagged against him, her hands clutching his shoulders, her head falling back, so that he dropped his arms about her again and held her to him, his mouth tasting the curve of her neck where it joined her shoulder beneath the open vee of her shirt. She moaned and trembled, her hands moving feverishly to his sides and down his body to his legs and up again. He thought he would explode. His need of her was so great, her answer to it so profound, that he could think of nothing but having her naked against him, wild with passion and returning his every touch.

He sank to his knees, carrying her with him, and her arms came around him, tightening as his mouth continued to explore the curve of her neck, dipping further beneath the fabric of her shirt. He pushed his hands between them, finding buckles and buttons and corresponding holes. Impatient, he loosened as many as his patience would allow and pulled at the nubby flannel. Suddenly his hands were full of the heavy, unbelievable softness of her breasts. She gasped and jerked violently. He dropped his hands, sure that he had hurt her, and his head came up, his arms reaching out to fold her against him. In that moment, she lifted her face to his, and what he saw there—the trust, the passion, the *innocence*—went straight to his heart like an arrow. He let his arms drop about her, not in embrace, but in surrender to that innocence.

She tilted her head, and he saw that her lovely hair was falling down, slipping in sleek, cloudy locks from the string that bound it. He caught it and took the string in his hand, letting it down about her shoulders.

"You are so incredibly beautiful," he said, and she smiled, her lids dropping demurely over her eyes. "I want to make love to you."

She lifted her chin and looked up at him, her eyes brimming and bright. "I know," she whispered, and her mouth opened again, but she closed it and shrugged, her gaze falling away.

"What?" he pressed gently, and she shrugged again, laying her hand flat against his chest.

"I don't know what to say to you."

He knew what he wanted to hear, but suddenly he also knew it wouldn't be enough. He sank back on his heels and took a deep, silent breath.

"Laney," he said carefully, "have you . . . have you ever . . . had a boyfriend?"

Her gaze zipped up to study his face, and he could see that she was unsure of his meaning. She rubbed her palms on her thighs. "Well, of course. Once in Casper, I dated the same guy every night for two whole weeks. My aunt was frantic. She thought I was going to do something stupid, and my parents would kill her."

"Did you?" he asked quickly. "Do something stupid, I mean."

She looked him squarely in the eyes. "No."

He lifted a hand to his forehead, not sure if he was grateful or disappointed. "I don't mean to pry . . ." he began, and she laughed easily.

"That's all right. I understand. There just isn't much to tell. There was one other fellow. You remind me of him in a way. We met in Seattle one weekend, but I was only nineteen, and he was in college. I couldn't stay there, and he couldn't come here. I guess he finally met someone else." She folded her hands and went on. "Lots of men who come here get it in their heads that I'm part of the package, you know? And I have to pretty much keep them in their places."

"They give you a hard time?" he asked.

"They try. But I don't give them much chance. I make sure they know, right away, that they can't take advantage of me, that they'd be lost out here without me, and that they can't talk me into anything. It's the only way I can do my job. Besides, most of them are married and those that aren't... Well, let's just say I never met anyone like you before."

Danzer pushed his hands over his face, trying to place everything that she had told him. Unless he very much missed his guess, her experience with men was limited to two weeks in Casper, Wyoming, a weekend in Seattle, Washington, and repelling—quite expertly, it would seem—the men who passed fleetingly through her parents' lodge. He didn't know if he was happy about that or not. When he'd thought she had a boyfriend he was sick, but the thought that she'd never...that he would be the first...

What, he wondered, had he let himself in for? Obviously she didn't take lightly the kind of encounter they'd just had, but for some reason she'd allowed it to happen, and should he press the advantage she'd given him, she'd surely respond with a depth of feeling and commitment he wasn't sure he could match.

What would it mean, loving a woman like this? The question was too weighty to answer without a great deal of thought, and he knew he was in no state of mind to even begin. He steeled himself, knowing he dared not touch her again, not now.

"Fix your hair," he said softly, offering her the string, "and button your shirt. We'd better get that wood before they come looking for us."

She nodded, a sweetness of expression on her face that registered neither disappointment nor relief. He got up and walked over to where she'd dropped the ax. Was he nuts, more decent than he knew, or just plain scared? he wondered. He bent and snatched up the ax by its red handle, unhappy with what he was thinking. Time would tell, he supposed, but as she joined him, her hair tied back and her clothing straightened, he knew quite well that it didn't have

ᴥ IT'S A ᴥ
SILHOUETTE HONEYMOON
A SWEETHEART
OF A FREE OFFER!

FOUR NEW SILHOUETTE ROMANCE™ NOVELS—FREE!

Take a "Silhouette Honeymoon" with four exciting romances—yours FREE from Silhouette Romance™ Each of these hot-off-the-press novels brings you all the passion and tenderness of today's greatest love stories . . . your free passport to a bright new world of love and adventure! But wait . . . there's even more to this great offer!

A LOVELY BRACELET WATCH— ABSOLUTELY FREE!

You'll love your elegant bracelet watch—this classic LCD quartz watch is a perfect expression of your style and good taste—and it's yours free as an added thanks for giving our Reader Service a try!

AN EXCITING MYSTERY BONUS—FREE!

With this offer, you'll also receive a special mystery bonus. You'll be thrilled with this surprise gift. It will be the source of many compliments as well as a useful and attractive addition to your home.

PLUS

SPECIAL EXTRAS—FREE!

When you join the Silhouette Reader Service, you'll get your free monthly newsletter, packed with news of your favorite authors and upcoming books.

FREE HOME DELIVERY!

Send for your Silhouette Romance novels and enjoy the convenience of previewing 6 new books every month, delivered right to your home. If you decide to keep them, pay just $2.25* per book—with no additional charges for home delivery. And you may cancel at any time, for any reason, just by sending us a note or a shipping statement marked "cancel" or by returning an unopened shipment to us at our expense. Either way the free books and gifts are yours to keep! Great savings plus total convenience add up to a sweetheart of a deal for you!

START YOUR SILHOUETTE HONEYMOON TODAY—
JST COMPLETE, DETACH & MAIL YOUR FREE OFFER CARD!

SILHOUETTE ROMANCE™

FREE OFFER CARD

4 FREE BOOKS

FREE HOME DELIVERY!

PLACE HEART STICKER HERE

FREE BRACELET WATCH

FREE FACT-FILLED NEWSLETTER!

PLUS AN EXTRA BONUS MYSTERY GIFT!

YES! Please send my 4 SILHOUETTE ROMANCE™ novels, free, along with my free Bracelet Watch and Mystery Gift! Then send me 6 SILHOUETTE ROMANCE™ novels every month and bill me just $2.25* per book with no additional charges for shipping and handling. If I'm not completely satisfied I can cancel at any time as outlined on the opposite page. The free books, Bracelet Watch and Mystery Gift remain mine to keep!   215 CIS HAX9

NAME _____
(please print)

ADDRESS _____ APT _____

CITY _____

STATE _____ ZIP _____

If offer card is missing, write to:
Silhouette Reader Service, 901 Fuhrmann Blvd., P.O. Box 1867, Buffalo, N.Y. 14269-1867

BUSINESS REPLY CARD

First Class   Permit No. 717   Buffalo, NY

Postage will be paid by addressee

Silhouette Books
901 Fuhrmann Blvd.
P.O. Box 1867
Buffalo, NY 14240-9952

NO POSTAGE
NECESSARY
IF MAILED
IN THE
UNITED STATES

anything to do with his moral character. With most of the women he'd known making love and being in love were two different things, but it wasn't like that this time. Somehow it just wasn't the same. He wanted her, and it was gratifying to know she wanted him, but was he ready for everything Laney had to offer? Could he take her body and reject her heart? He didn't think so, and he had too much to do to be in love. Too much adventure waited for him, too much experience. He was on a quest, and that was what mattered, wasn't it? Well, wasn't it?

Chapter Six

Come on, princess, don't cry."

Danzer wiped the big, sparkling tears from Annie's face. They'd gone through a similar scene the day before with little Mike, but Danzer had soon talked him into a better mood. He had a way with children, and it seemed natural to let him deal with Annie now. The child bit her lip and caught one of her tight, yellow braids in a damp fist.

"I-I don't w-w-wanna go."

Danzer knelt on the rough planking of the pier, the others in an anxious group behind him, and took her into his arms. "I know, sweetie, but your mom and dad must be missing you something awful by now. Don't you want to see them just a little bit?" She nodded her head, pulling her braid like a bell cord. "That's my girl. Besides, you'll be back next summer. Won't that be great?"

A first, tentative smile curved her lips. "W-will you be h-here?"

He cleared his throat and cast a guilty look over his shoulder. "I don't know," he finally said. "Let's hope so, 'cause I sure wouldn't want to miss you." That seemed to mollify her. She stuck her little finger into her mouth and curled her other arm about his neck. A collective sigh went up from the general group, and Laney stepped forward to add her voice.

"I'm going with you this time," she said. "Won't that be fun? We can talk and play games all the way home."

"And maybe you won't barf all over the plane," Kevin put in.

"Of course she won't," Lillian hurried to assure them both. "Why, you're a pair of seasoned fliers now."

"That's right," Danzer agreed, standing with the child in his arms. "And we'd better get flying right now or we'll be late for our second connection."

There was a flurry of goodbyes and see-you-soons, then an eager Kevin boarded, followed by Laney in denim jeans and jacket over a gauzy, dark orange shirt with an up-turned collar. Danzer handed Annie inside to Laney's waiting arms, and for the first time in days they did not fly apart upon such innocent contact. The previous day's trip to deliver the Petty boys to their home had helped to steady their now-awkward relationship a bit, but the tension was still evident. For a moment their eyes met, and Laney enjoyed a brief, calm instant before the uneasiness again filled his gaze. She looked away, wishing to be neither the giver nor the receiver of his discomfort.

Ever since the camping trip, Danzer had been quieter than usual and much more distant. At times, Laney was certain that it was for the better and felt a kind of relief. On other occasions, however, she found her mood one of petulance and inexplicable desperation over his seeming lack of consideration. The memory of his kiss was likewise dual. Hours would go by wherein she would smugly assure herself that she was cured of any desire for him. But then, unexpectedly, she would be assailed by memories of his mouth and hands and body sweeping over her. Such memories would be so clear, she imagined they were actually kissing. She felt like a coin constantly coming up heads when she expected tails and vice versa. She couldn't guess upon which she would land when they were alone together again, as they would be for a lengthy period in the afternoon. First they would fly to Miles City, where they would deliver the kids, and then to Helena, where they were to meet a party of hunters eager to make the first day of the fall black bear season. She couldn't help wondering what the day would hold.

Like Laney's feelings, the day proved full of contrasts. On the long trip from the mountain lodge to the flat plains of Custer County, Laney was occupied with caring for the children. Little Annie did suffer a short period of nausea, but everyone was grateful that the second experience was so much less miserable than the first. Before too long, Laney was able to concentrate on word games and singing rather than nursing care, and even Danzer joined in with a deep stirring bass on some of the more familiar tunes. She convinced herself that the day would be normal and uneventful. They said farewell to the children at Miles City and, after refueling, stepped into a local grocery to stock up on soft drinks and snacks for the return trip.

She couldn't decide from a selection that included a bag of chips, packaged cakes and an array of fruit. The fruit was, of course, the far wiser choice, but junk food was so scarce in her secluded little part of the world that she could hardly resist. She settled on the chips, then abandoned them for the cakes, but she couldn't decide between strawberry and chocolate fillings, so she told herself to be wise and choose the fruit, then the idea of the chips intruded again, and she started all over. Danzer watched the whole process first with confusion then humor, and "for the sake of the schedule" he came up with a solution: he simply bought a dozen of everything, including a variety of fruits and a pound of smoked sausage to be sliced and eaten with a box of crackers, plus a chocolate bar each! Laney was both appalled and thrilled, but she warned him that she'd make him pay for every pound she gained as a result of his largess.

"You don't have anything to worry about," he told her dismissively. "You're a fast metabolizer; you'll work it off in no time. Besides, ninety percent of the women in this world would kill to look like you *with* an extra ten pounds."

She knew a compliment when she heard one, but she felt duty-bound to protest that he was spending too much money on pure junk. He gave her a look that seemed to ask on which planet she'd been living, then said offhandedly that she should not worry about it. She noted, however, that he struggled with a small smile afterward, and that seemed odd, but later on she forgot it in the sheer joy of gluttony.

The second leg of the flight seemed shorter than the first, and Laney was satisfied with the polite camaraderie they seemed to find. They ate and ate and clowned and teased and at least part of the time howled with laughter. There were comfortable silences interspersed with shallow, joking banter and periods of responsible work while charts were checked and landmarks sited to ensure they were on course. At one point, fully sated, Laney actually napped. When she came back to the co-pilot's seat a half hour later, yawning and tousled, a seriousness filled Dan's eyes, and he let slip a softly voiced, "You *are* beautiful." Touched, she couldn't sit there after that and excused herself to pull a comb through her hair and let her pulsing nerves calm. When she returned, the uneasiness she feared did not materialize. Instead, he seemed lighthearted and relaxed, much as before, and she found herself responding in the same manner.

They actually got to Helena earlier than they expected and found to their chagrin a message had been left for them at the airport. Their party would be delayed approximately three hours. On a whim, they caught a ride into town with an airline employee who was taking a couple of hours off to have dinner with his wife on her birthday. The restaurant where they planned to meet was in a section of town called Reeder's Alley. A carefully restored throwback to Helena's early days, the area was a favorite tourist attraction and leisure spot. There were boutiques and galleries to keep them entertained while they passed the extra hours.

Laney would have been content with window shopping, but Danzer Wilson was obviously a bird of a different feather. To her initial dismay, he seemed intent on buying everything he laid his hands on. The first purchase was not one but *two* sets of beautifully painted plates depicting the wildlife for which Montana is so famous, everything from the black bear to the mountain lion, including the grizzly, bighorn sheep, deer, antelope, moose and elk. One set he intended to present to her mother for a gift; the other he wanted himself as a "remembrance." From there he progressed to bubble bath packaged in a clever glass box, which he had wrapped and mailed to Annie. Then he purchased several leather working kits, one each for Kevin, Mark, Matt and Mike. For Hiram, he bought a hand-carved miniature mining camp inspired by the Gold Rush days and peopled with exquisitely detailed miners no taller than an inch. Laney was appalled at the cost of it all. And when Danzer came up with a pair of pure gold, uniquely crafted chains and elk's tooth pendants for the two of them, she was shocked into vehement protestation, which he laughed aside all too easily.

She could not countenance his behavior, and a plethora of suspicions crowded into her mind. She pictured him as everything from bank robber to compulsive shopper, from embezzler to pretender to the crown, *any* crown. Nothing she imagined squared with her lifelong association with Spartanism. She simply couldn't conceive of spending any amount of money over a very few dollars without careful planning, consideration and anticipation, sometimes years of it! The casualness and glee with which he just walked into a place and bought whatever he wanted without a moment's thought was foreign to her—and dangerously exciting. It occurred to her, not for the first time, that she actually knew very little about this man; yet she trusted him. He was a paradox to her.

That long gold chain about her neck felt both luxuriously indulgent and sinfully extravagant. It was only with protest that she even allowed him to slip it over her head, but once she dropped it inside her shirt and felt that heavy gold "tooth" slip into the cleft between her breasts, she felt a certain secret rightness. She knew it was destined to be one of her treasures, and that she would feel a certain thrill every time she looked at it, followed perhaps by a bittersweet memory of titillation and affection.

They made their way to the restaurant where the man and his wife were dining with a group of friends and took a table for themselves. Danzer ordered coffee and a full-course dinner for each of them, extravagant to the last. He laughed at her and insisted that extravagance was not the norm for him. He blamed it on her, saying she inspired him to excess, and she found herself happy with that idea, though the thought of all that money being spent troubled her.

When the man and his wife appeared at their table for introductions, Danzer somehow omitted Laney's surname, and the woman assumed, quite naturally, that they were married. Laney's face burned with embarrassment when Danzer carefully informed her otherwise, and the tempo of the evening abruptly changed to one of stilted unease. It remained so throughout the conclusion of their meal and the ride back to the airport.

The couple were friendly and talkative, and though Danzer managed a low-key response to their overtures, Laney could not bring herself to actively participate in the chit-chat. She was not skilled in that sort of thing and truthfully had no desire to be, but she would have liked to have been able to represent herself as completely unaffected by Danzer's little gaffe: the fact that she could not disturbed her more than anything else.

Laney was greatly relieved when the man checked his watch and announced that it was time to go. Taking his momentary leave of them, he escorted his wife back to their friends. She was an attractive woman, slender and fashionable in a lavender print chemise, her pale hair bobbed at chin-length, her shapely legs accented by a pair of delicate high-heeled sandals. She made Laney feel tacky and masculine in her denim and loafers. As he took his leave, the man wrapped his wife in his arms and kissed her. Laney turned away abruptly, her eyes colliding with Danzer's.

"They seem happy together, don't they?" he said in that same chatty voice he'd used with them. Laney tried to act natural, aloof.

"Yes. They seem to be an ideal couple."

"Aren't many of those around," he went on, but this time she merely nodded, her eyes trained on the remains of her salad. "Reminds me of Hi and Lillian."

A feeling of warmth and pride flooded her. There *was* something special between them. She wondered suddenly if she would ever have that something special with a man, and her eyes went automatically to Danzer's face. He seemed to be adrift with his own thoughts. She shifted her gaze, telling herself that she knew far too little about this man. Physical attraction, however compelling, did not necessarily lead to love, nor love to marriage. And she couldn't believe the path her thoughts were taking! By the time the man returned and they rose to join him, she was too tense and distracted even to respond when spoken to.

The drive back to the airport was filled with the same idle chatter as their meeting over dinner. The man seemed a good sort, and it was easy to see that he was proud of his wife. Danzer made a good listener, but Laney could only be grateful when they reached the trip's end.

"Thanks so much," Danzer said after getting out of the car. "I wish you'd let me buy you a tank of gasoline, though."

The man shook his head. "No, I didn't go out of my way at all. You can buy me a cup of coffee next time you're down this way."

"Be glad to."

Danzer shook the man's hand and watched him disappear behind a door marked for entrance by airport personnel only.

"Guess we'd better find our party," Laney said, handing back the packages she'd taken for him. Danzer nodded.

"Tell you what. I'll take these out and stow them away; you go on and look for our errant passengers. I'll catch up with you as soon as I'm sure the plane and the drum have been refueled."

Laney was a bit relieved to go her own way for a time. The experiences of this day were seriously troubling her. It hadn't been easy for her to admit how deeply she was attracted to him, and she had shocked herself that day on the mountain. She couldn't quite believe even now how eagerly she had given herself over to the passion. Once she had admitted to herself what she wanted, the wall between them had seemed to just crumble, unleashing desires she hadn't even known she had. She was glad they'd stopped, grateful that Danzer had not pressed. Yet, at any given moment, that feeling of absolute rightness would swamp her again, and she'd remember with startling clarity the sensations of his lovemaking.

Determinedly she pushed aside her thoughts and made her way to the private waiting area where they'd been told their group would be directed upon landing. She pulled the door open and let the smell of stale tobacco escape. Loud, raucous, male laughter greeted her, followed swiftly by the odor of strong drink. She stepped inside and took her measure of them. Four men gaped at her. Three were sprawled in various angles over the aluminum and navy-blue vinyl chairs, while a fourth stood, a highball glass in his hand and a cigar between his teeth. All were dressed casually, all were drinking, and there were obvious signs of money: expensive watches, new clothing, overlarge rings and belt buckles, not to mention the mountain of gear stacked in one corner.

"Well, well." The one standing removed his stinking cigar from his teeth and addressed her presence. "What have we here? Don't tell me you're the pilot Scott sent to meet us. I'm just not that lucky!"

The others laughed and made comments she chose not to hear. She walked into the center of the small room and gave each one a frank, unintimidated look. "You're right," she said, "you're not that lucky. I'm Laney Scott."

"The wife?" one wanted to know, as if it were unthinkable a man should send his woman in his place.

"The daughter," she corrected bluntly, and he exchanged a speculative look with his seatmate. Laney knew that look, it expressed lewdness and disrespect. His manner was meant to intimidate her. She knew it had to be countered. She hung her thumbs in the belt loops of her jeans.

"So you tough guys want to go after bear, huh? Better make it Teddy Bear."

"Whoa!" The chorus went up all around. Backs straightened. Smirks went back and forth. The man with the cigar tapped the ashes off the end.

"Lady, for your information, this group has safaried in Africa."

"Really?" She grinned sweetly. "Let me guess. Hot days, cool nights, cots, tents, Land Rovers and half-a-dozen porters to do everything but pull the trigger." She knew from the blank looks that she wasn't far from right. Truth be told, she envied them for their jaunt through Africa, but she wasn't about to let them know that. "Well, welcome to the Rockies, gentlemen," she said. "I hope you can walk all day, tote your own gear, eat out of a can and sleep on the ground. You won't bathe until you get back or remove your shoes except to change your socks. Everything that's exposed will burn during the day and freeze during the night. Everything that's covered will itch, but you won't scratch: your hands will be full, and when they're not, you won't have the energy. You'll climb rock sheer as glass and so broken and sharp it'll cut your hands and face and the rubber bottoms of your three-hundred-dollar boots. And after all that you'll be lucky if you so much as sight a bear, let alone a legal one. If one of you should manage to make a kill—and I do mean *if*—then you'll have to cape it according to strict regulations, stake it, dry it, roll it and carry it back down the mountain. After it's been checked by a ranger and passed, you can worry about getting it home."

The man with the cigar was looking worried already. "And if it doesn't pass?" he wanted to know. Laney smiled.

"It'll pass. Your guide will see to that."

He exchanged glances with the others. "Listen here now, we've spent a lot of money on this trip. We expect results. We pay, we kill."

"You pay, you take your chances," she told him flatly. She scanned the group. "Any of you don't like that, you'd better take the next flight back to wherever you came from. That's a wilderness up there, and *it* can kill *you*, if you don't show the proper respect. If you do as you're told, you'll get through just fine, and maybe you'll even have a trophy to show for your efforts. Then you can brag around the country club about what mountain men you are. But get it into your head that you know best up there, and the only bragging being done will be at your eulogy."

She let that sink in, and it seemed to be having the desired effect, until the least responsive of the four suddenly lurched to his feet and made a dismissive gesture with his hand. One whiff told her he had had too much to drink.

"Ah, what does she know?" He slurred the words. "She's nothin' but a skirt in jeans. She could sure warm a sleeping bag, though."

"But not yours," said a deep, commanding voice, and every eye turned to the doorway. Danzer Wilson let it close behind him. He looked big and tough and confident, his handsome face composed, his stance rigid, his arms loose at his sides. He gave the drunk a thorough once-over, from head to toe and back again. "You couldn't handle it, anyway. And for your information, Laney probably knows as much about these mountains as any man alive. At any rate, her license says she's capable and professional, and on the hunt, she's boss. Period. But should she find herself *outnumbered*, shall we say, all she has to do is crook her little finger, and there I'll be. Understood?" Laney smothered a smile amid stuttered assurances and throat clearings. Danzer nodded just once.

"Shoulder your gear," he said. "We've clearance to take off in twenty minutes." Without another word, he turned and opened the door, lifting a hand to Laney in invitation. She calmly walked out, Danzer immediately following. A scurry for packs and bags erupted behind them.

"Damn it, Chuck," someone complained, "if you're going to get your face broken, do it falling off a mountain, will you? I'd like a chance to get my money's worth before we have to haul you off to the hospital."

Laney bit her lip to keep from laughing and hurried along the corridor to the heavy glass door that led directly onto the tarmac. By the time they reached it, the men had spilled out into the hallway and begun lugging their gear in that direction. She pushed on through and held the door for Danzer. The sun had disappeared behind the crest line. The night was less than an hour away.

"They aren't all like that, are they?" he asked as they walked toward the plane.

"Not all," she answered, halting him with a hand placed in the bend of his elbow. He gave her a quizzical look. "Thanks for what you said in there."

"Anytime."

"It wasn't necessary, but I appreciate it anyway. No one else has ever done anything like that for me."

"My pleasure."

"I just wanted you to know."

He smiled, and on pure impulse Laney stepped closer and went up on tiptoe to place a kiss on his cheek. It was scratchy with the dark shadow of beard that she found rakishly attractive, and she touched her hand to the other jaw, conscious of the men hauling their gear out onto the tarmac. She let herself down, and Danzer turned his head to look at the quartet making their way toward them. Suddenly he switched his gaze to her face, and she felt his strong hands close around her upper arms. He pulled her against him, and his mouth came down over hers, his arms sliding around her. For a long breathless moment, he held her, his mouth claiming hers possessively, until the need seemed to drain out of him and he gradually released her.

Laney had to steady herself to keep from swaying. The feel of his mouth on hers still burned, and she felt branded where his hands had clutched her. Now it was her turn to be puzzled. She stared up at him, any word she might have said forestalled by the approach of the others. He set his mouth apologetically, brows dipping low over eyes that didn't quite meet hers. A muscle twitched in the flat of his jaw. It was as if he'd staked a public claim and then immediately thought better of it.

"We'd better hurry," he whispered, and she nodded in agreement, choosing to treat the whole thing as if it hadn't really happened. But it had, and she knew even as she walked silently by his side that it was just one more episode she wouldn't be able to forget, one more moment that would return to haunt her in the dead of night and challenge what little sense she had remaining. And try as she might, she couldn't quite help the small burgeoning of pride that broke in her when she thought of those other men. Not one of them, not all of them together was a match for Danzer Wilson, whoever or whatever he might be, and they knew it. Could such a man truly love her? She put the thought away and smiled at him, her cool, poised exterior a perfect foil for the emotions trembling inside.

"Why don't you come along, Danzer boy? You've broken trail before. You could be a help. Besides, didn't you say you took this job so you could get in some huntin' and fishin'? Not that you can make a kill. The law's real strict on licensin' bear kills. But, shoot, the trackin' is the real fun, anyhow. I could teach you a thing or two."

Danzer smiled gratefully at Hiram Scott, then scanned the other four faces at the table. He hadn't made any friends with that little speech of his—except maybe one, and he didn't want to think about her, not just now. His mind got all boggled up when he thought about her, and it was even worse when he was with her. He didn't want to lead her on, but sometimes he just couldn't keep his hands off her. She got to him in the strangest way, and he got the oddest pleasure out of doing little things for her, like buying her junk food and necklaces. He couldn't quite figure out why he did those things. Maybe the answer was to not be with her, to clear her out of his mind so he could think rationally again.

"I'd like to go along, Hi, provided Weir and his friends here have no objections."

Hi put the question to them. "What do you say, Mr. Weir? You boys object to having my man along?"

The one named Chuck rubbed a hand against the back of his head and slid a careful look at Danzer. He cleared his throat. "Um, that, uh, woman. She's not, uh, coming along, is she?"

"Who, Laney?" Hi grinned and laid a finger alongside his nose. "Naw, we take turns, Laney and me. She'll take out the next party, and I'll stay home and enjoy Mother's cookin'. It's just us men this time around."

Chuck relaxed visibly, as did Weir, who spat out the butt end of his cigar into one of Lillian's saucers. "Sure the fly boy can come along," he said heartily. "Hey, the more the merrier, I say."

"Yeah," Chuck joined in, "we're friendly. He's welcome."

"Sure. No problem," the others echoed.

Danzer glanced over his shoulder. Laney and her mother sat before the hearth her father had built with his own hands. They were looking at the plates he'd given Lillian and talking quietly. Laney's elk's tooth necklace was outside her shirt, and she was holding the pendant in her hand like a talisman. He wondered if anybody had ever given her an impromptu present before—just because, just for fun, on account of her smile and her frown and the look in those pale, bright eyes. He wondered if he should have been the one, and he thought about his sudden need to claim her in front of these men, to mark her as his private territory.

"Danzer?"

He turned back, the looks on their faces telling him he'd missed something.

"What?"

"The hunt. It's settled, right?"

"Oh, right."

Hiram grinned and tilted his head to one side in order to bring his wife and daughter into view over Danzer's shoulder. *He knows,* Danzer thought. *God, he knows I want to make love to his daughter.*

"Guess that's it then," Weir said, working a kink out of his back.

"Might as well get some sleep," Hi said by way of agreement. "We'll wait 'til midday to set out, but it's goin' to be a busy mornin'. Good night, gents."

He stood astraddle the bench and stretched. The others followed suit, the four hunters wandering away to climb the stairs.

"Mother," Hiram called. "This old bear's ready to hibernate. You comin'?"

Lillian got up off the floor, the plates boxed once more and in hand. "I'm going to put them up on the wall," she said to Danzer as she drew near, her smile proof of her pleasure. "You shouldn't have done it, but they're so lovely. And that necklace, Laney says you bought a pair."

Danzer caught a quick breath. "Well, we both liked them."

"And the carving, those tiny people and all that detail," she went on.

"I've never seen anything like that," Hiram put in. "Sure enough, nobody ever gave me anything like it before, but you shouldn't be spendin' your money on us, boy. You shame us, we pay you so little."

"That's got nothing to do with it, Hi. I told you, I didn't come here for the money. I came for the experience, and it's been that, let me tell you."

"Just the same," the older man said, holding out his arm for his wife to come, "it's mighty thoughtful, and let that be the end of it."

"Yes sir. Good night." He shook Hiram's hand and gave Lillian a hug. The couple went out, Hi yawning and Lillian holding her painted plates. Danzer turned, knowing full well that Laney was still there. She rose and came to meet him at the foot of the stairs.

"I heard," she said simply. "You need anything? Gear, I mean. I've got a telescoping rod you could fit in your pack. Might get in a little fishing."

"Thanks," he said. "Sounds good."

"You need anything else? We're licensed outfitters, you know. We've got at least one of everything. I was thinking of this little first-aid kit we keep. It might come in handy."

He shook his head. "Thanks anyway, I have one."

She seemed to have run out of things to say, and he felt a tightening in his body that told him he ought to get away while he could.

"Sleep well," he said. "See you in the morning."

He started up the stairs, aware that she stayed behind.

"I can't figure you out," she said, stopping him about the third or fourth step. He turned, trading hands on the rough pine banister.

"What do you mean?"

"You spent money like water today, yet your salary's hardly snail spit."

He shrugged and lifted a brow. "I just happen to have a little money, that's all. Like I said . . ."

"I know. I know. You came for the experience. But that doesn't add up, either. A man with a little money can buy himself experience, just like Weir and those others."

"I'm not like Weir and those others," he said. "They're after trophy, bragging rights. I want to experience another way of life. You can't buy that. You have to *do* it."

"Makes sense," she decided at length. "Makes good sense. If I had a little money, I'd like to do that myself."

That surprised him. "Really? I thought you loved it here."

"Oh, I do, but..." She couldn't seem to find the right words. "Things are changing," she said at last. "I can feel it. I've been feeling it ever since you came here. I think that's why I didn't like you at first, and ... I'm sorry about that."

He fought the impulse to walk back down to her—he went so far, even, to take that first step, but halted. "That's okay," he said, wishing his voice didn't sound quite so strained. "What's a little fish guts between friends?"

She laughed, and he thought it was the first time since he'd rolled the plane for her that her laughter had sounded so genuine, so warm. It made him want to kiss her, made him think of having her beneath him in his bed and seeing the rapture on her face. But Laney wouldn't... She wasn't made for... He came to the truth suddenly: she would expect more of him than any other woman ever had. He wasn't sure he was ready for that. He wasn't sure he would ever be ready.

"Well, good night," he said and turned away.

"Good night, Dan," she replied, her voice low and rich. He could feel her watching him, following his every step with her eyes, but he just kept climbing.

You're either a sage or a flat damn fool, he told himself, and when he turned onto the landing and looked back down at her, standing there with her soft orange blouse clinging to the full curve of her breasts and bringing fiery highlights into her hair, he figured it was the latter. But he dared not go back down to her, not with his fool's body urging it, not

with that honest doubt in mind, not with that mantle of re-
gal innocence she wore beneath the cape of her pride and
ability. He lifted a hand in a final leave-taking and went to
his room.

Chapter Seven

Laney swished the broom back and forth over the rough stone floor, oblivious to the fact that she was merely rearranging the dirt rather than removing it. Her mother stopped stacking the dishes in the cabinet and watched, dry hands embroiling themselves in the front of her apron out of habit.

"That broom's going to be nothing but a stub by the time you finish that."

"Yes, Mama," Laney agreed absently, confused when her mother laughed. "I'm sorry, Mama, what'd you say?"

Lillian stepped forward and took the broom handle from her daughter's hands, a knowing smile on her face.

"I used to be that way when your dad would leave me," she said. "I'd moon and mope and worry."

"I'm not worried, Mama," Laney said, reaching for the broom again. "Dad can take care of himself out there. I'm not worried at all." Lillian put the broom aside gently, her face serious now.

"You in love with him, Laney?"

She could have pretended shock, could have played dumb.
But she just didn't have it in her. The days without him had
exhausted her. She was exhausted from waiting, from longing, and it had been not five months or five weeks, but five
days. Five lousy days. She folded her arms protectively
about her middle and allowed herself an honest answer.

"I don't know, Mama. Sometimes I think I must be.
Sometimes..." She shook her head. "I just don't know."

Lillian put on a sad face, but beneath it was the prag-
matic understanding natural to mothers the world over. "I'd
hoped it would be as easy for you as it was for your papa
and me."

"You had no doubts then?" Laney questioned.

"Of course I had doubts, but my certainty was so much
stronger, and never when I was with him, never when we
were together."

The answer did not satisfy Laney. She sighed audibly, and
her mother chucked her beneath the chin, as she'd done so
often when Laney was small. "Give it time. Follow your
instincts. You two are a lot different. Maybe that's the
problem."

Laney tried to be comforted. She attempted a smile.
"What you said about following my instincts, Crater said
the very same thing."

"And who knows you better than Crater?"

Laney nodded. Somehow, no one knew her better than
that scratchy old man. It was a mystery to her how they
connected, but connect they did, and that connection was a
vital part of her, a strong, steadying part. She would miss
him. The unbidden thought startled her. She cocked her
head sharply to one side, her green eyes narrowing to slits.
Was she actually considering leaving?

"Do you ever think of leaving here, Mama?"

Lillian took the broom in hand, all business now. "I certainly do. I always have. Oh, for the most part I've been happy here. It's been a good life—unconventional, but good. The thing is, there's so much else, Laney, easier places. I'll always want to come back here, summers maybe or holidays when the snow lies heavy on those mountaintops and spills down into our valley. But I wouldn't want you to stay on here for all your life, Laney. There's so much out there you can't even imagine, and it's not as easy here as it used to be. You don't get so much for your effort, seems like."

She'd never heard her mother speak like this before, and she herself had never entertained such ideas until recently, but it struck a chord in her now. Were her instincts telling her that she belonged with Danzer Wilson, that her life lay away from here at his side? Or was the message simply that she was primed for change and her feelings for Danzer were a symptom of it?

"Don't fret yourself, child. Go on out and wait for him. It won't be long now, and when he comes, maybe you'll know, maybe it'll all come clear."

Laney smiled and hugged her mother. "Thank you, Mama."

Lillian patted her back, chuckling. "Might as well," she said, "you're not doing any good in here."

Laney kissed her and went out. She always seemed to think better in the sunshine, or maybe it was that she didn't think at all. There were times, she knew, when she operated purely on instinct, when intellect and reason had nothing to do with function and performance. It was like autopilot, automatic response. Those were times of great freedom for her, when she felt a oneness with the world around her. She sought it now, gradually, letting it slip over her like the air over her skin.

It was getting late in the year for shorts, but she'd worn cutoffs anyway, expecting to stay in most of the morning. The day was still crisp enough to hold a faint chill, and she felt autumn on her bare legs and face and hands. It was glorious.

She paused at the woodpile and put one foot up at a time, folding down her thick white socks and checking the ties on her athletic shoes. She pushed up the sleeves of her pale blue cardigan and pulled a string from the breast pocket of her white T-shirt to tie up her hair. This last thing she did as she wandered toward the low, weathered barn.

Lillian had milked the cow this morning as usual and fed the calf they were fattening for slaughter, but she'd left the chickens in. They were spooked. Something had excited them, and there were tracks. She had thought maybe a big dog or a wolf, though they'd not had that kind of visit before. Hi had sworn, years ago, to have seen a whole pack high up on the fringe of the snowy slopes, but it seemed unlikely these days. Laney had found dog tracks before, and Crater had spoken of a small pack that had tried to take down a big old grizzly and been ripped and tromped for it. Maybe it was one of them.

She took a bucket of feed from the bin in the shed and carried it over to the hen yard. She sat it down by the gate and carefully walked the perimeter. Dog tracks, she decided, just one but big, and it limped on the right rear leg. Probably hurt and hungry, poor thing. She wondered if any of the working ranches to the east had lost a dog and if it would be back to spook the chickens. She let herself inside the enclosure, carefully latched the tall gate and walked the few steps to the hen house. Everything seemed calm. She lifted the bar and pushed the door in.

"Here, chick-chick-chick. Come and get it, chick-chick-chick."

They seemed content in the darkness of the low, wir
dowless structure. She stepped back and spread a little grain
Soon one greedy old girl sidled through, then another rur
fled and squawked, and soon they were fluttering toward the
door. Emperor, the imperious, dark red rooster, made
dead run, wings tucked, head high. Laney stepped aside and
gave him room. He was known to peck bare legs. She scat
tered the remaining grain and slipped inside to steal the eggs
There were five. One of the girls hadn't laid. Probably ha
to do with that dog sniffing around. She hoped it didn'
come back, hoped it would find its way home and not sta
out here and grow wild and mean, if it hadn't already.

She pushed the door back on the inside and blocked it s
it wouldn't accidentally swing shut, then she checked th
water and let herself out, fighting off Emperor with kick
and stomps. He always wanted through that gate, alway
wanted out in the wide world. He had a nice, safe little hom
here, half a dozen hens to lord it over and all the food an
drink he could need. Yet he wanted to go adventuring. An
imals weren't so different from people.

She started back to the house, the bucket swinging gentl
from her hand, her mind at rest for the moment. She passe
the low, grayed outbuildings one by one—the grain shed, th
little barn, the toolshed, the warehouse where they store
their gear. She stepped into the little clearing between th
row of outbuildings and the woodpile, heading for th
house. A whistle sounded, two notes sharp and low, and i
was as if every nerve ending in her body suddenly switche
on. She whipped around, eyes searching the canopy of tree
along the lower slope, heart pounding like a locomotive
There! Two, three patches of bright hunter's orange flash
ing through the trees. She left the bucket with the eggs or
the chopping block and started running.

She met them at the timberline. Danzer came first, and
then Weir, followed by her father and the others. Danze

waved, and Hi cut a caper, hollering something nonsensical. It had been a good hunt, a good time. She laughed and sped up her trot, meeting him about two hundred yards out. He hadn't shaved, and a dark, heavy stubble covered his jaws and chin and upper lip. He hurried to meet her, all flushed and smiling.

"Laney!" he called, and she couldn't help the surge of joy she felt. The eagerness in his voice sent a white bolt like sunshine through her.

"Dan!"

She threw both arms around him in a crushing, exuberant hug. He was laughing hard and trying to keep his balance, while everybody else talked at once.

"Damn fine trophy!"

"Big old she-bear..."

"Tracked her two days..."

"One clean shot..."

"Took all five of us to skin her out!"

She gave her father the same greeting as Dan and listened to him snort, knowing full well she'd been too obvious. Would Danzer think she was pushy? Well, he'd kissed her in front of these men, hadn't he? She reminded herself that he'd also kept his distance afterward. It was all so terribly confusing.

As if sensing her turmoil, Dan slipped an arm around her waist and propelled her along in front of the others, his smile a recurring flash of white teeth against the rough beard and darkened skin of his face. They made that uncomfortable small talk that two people make when they don't want to say what's really on their minds.

It was great, he told her, rough but great. The scenery was beautiful, and in many ways it was like going back in time, but he wouldn't want to live like that. "Neither would I," she heard herself say, and instantly thought of Crater. A kind of guilt descended and immediately rose again. Dan talked on.

What had she done? he wanted to know. Nothing but clean house and fish a little? Something had riled the chickens, huh? A big dog? They'd seen one. It was in pretty bad shape, but big, big as a wolf, only black. She hoped it wouldn't come back. He told her not to worry. It had been wounded, and the wound was deep and festered. Hi had put it out of its misery. He sounded genuinely sorry, and she'd never felt so happy and sad all at the same time. If this was love... She checked the thought, but it came creeping back. If this was love, let it come, let it be. Just let it go both ways.

They reached the house before the others, and they paused before the door, looking deeply into each other's eyes. Laney smiled up at him, feeling shy and bold in the same moment. She let her hand travel up and release the clip in the center of his chest that allowed him to open the harness of his pack. He slipped it off one arm at a time, and she helped him, knowing it was heavy. They left it on the ground beside the door, eyes only for each other. He lifted a hand and skimmed a knuckle across her cheek.

"You've been hiding a pair of great legs," he commented softly, and she laughed, expecting anything but that. "I'm glad to be back."

"Bet you're tired."

He made a face. "Either that or I'm dying an inch at a time."

The others came up then, Hi issuing instructions about storing the hide, packs dropping like hundred-pound weights. They opened the door and went in. Lil came running and patted Danzer and hugged Hi, exclaiming about the gray bristle on his chin.

"You'll be wanting a good meal," she said.

"Yes, ma'am!" It was unanimous.

"Steaks and potatoes," she said, to groans of anticipation. "There's plenty of time to clean up, and time for a nap, if you feel the need. There's cinnamon cakes and coffee in the dining room. Laney, did you get all those beds made up?"

"Almost, Mama." She felt a smile trying to get out and squelched it. "I'll finish up right away."

The party broke up, some opting for immediate showers, others for unpacking. The coffee and cakes would come later.

"That nap sounds best to me," Danzer said, and Laney's heart leaped. "I'll be going on up. If the smell of those steaks doesn't wake me, I'm too far gone, so just let me be."

"Well, I'm for cleaning up," said Hi. "Then after that, old girl, me and you are gonna slip off up to the piney woods for a private talk." He had his arms around his wife, and he rubbed his stubbly chin against her cheek. She slapped at him and scolded him fondly for his boldness, while Danzer laughed and shook his head and Laney watched with color glowing in her cheeks.

"Just for that, I'm going out to tend to my hens, you old rascal," Lil declared.

"Oh, Mama," said Laney, "the eggs are on the chopping block. I already let them out and fed them."

"Then I'll put them up again," Lil snapped. She shook a finger at her husband. "There's been a beast sniffing around, and I'll not have it get my good layers!"

"Well, I'd better go along then," Hi said with mock gravity. A smile twitched on Lillian's mouth.

"I guess you'd better."

"This is getting too graphic for me," said Dan, and he went out laughing.

"You two," Laney told them, "are worse than a couple of kids."

"You make that bed," Lillian chided, and Laney grinned.

"Yes, Mama."

They went out, pinching and poking at one another. Laney went to the linen closet below the staircase and took out a set of sheets and a pillow slip. She passed two men on the staircase as they went down to the shower, clean clothing and razors in their hands. Laney nodded and went on up, her heart pounding. The house was essentially empty, except for her and Danzer, and that was disconcerting. She strolled along the landing, the clean linens heavy in her arms, telling herself this had been unintentional, unplanned. She hadn't made his bed earlier because the sheets needed to be changed, and she hadn't already changed them because her mind had been elsewhere. She almost believed it, not that it mattered.

She shifted the weight of the linens to her hip and listened at his door. A curious buzzing came from inside. What was he doing in there? There was one sure way to find out. She raised her fist and knocked on the door. The buzz stopped abruptly. Two seconds later, he opened up and stared out at her. A lump formed in Laney's throat. He'd removed his shirt, and a fine spread of dark hair covered his upper chest and dwindled to a narrow line that disappeared below the waistband of his jeans. She thought of that night she'd caught him coming out of the shower. He had apparently just turned off the water when she'd entered the room, and she hadn't known he was there until he'd walked out with only that towel around his waist. She still remembered how he'd looked, glistening wet, all but naked, and male, totally male. When he'd washed her foot, things had happened to her that she still couldn't describe. Imagine, something like that from a little foot rub. Suddenly she realized he was speaking.

"Uh, wh-what?"

He held a battery-powered electric razor in his hand and had already cut a wide swath in the five-day-old beard. "I said, did you want something?"

"Oh. C-can I come in?" She was painfully aware of the thickening in her throat and attempted to clear it away. "I need to make your bed."

He stared at her and scratched his chin, a mischievous smile playing at his mouth. "Make my bed? What do you think this is, a hotel?"

She picked up on the bantering tone and returned it. "All right, all right, I deserved that. Now do you want your sheets changed or not?"

"Do," he said, stepping aside; then, as she slipped by, "I hope you won't expect a tip."

She shot him a warning look that almost concealed her amusement. "I can always just leave the linens and go."

"Oh, no. No, no." He closed the door as if for emphasis. "You go right ahead and do your thing. I'll just finish mowing down this beard." He walked across the floor on bare feet and stood before the small mirror hung at eye level.

She smiled at his back and placed the folded linens on the bedside table. The razor hummed and buzzed as he moved it over his chin. Laney removed the pillowcase and slipped on the fresh one, remembering the last time she'd done this. She hadn't been wrong. Danzer Wilson had brought change. Even her feelings toward him had changed. Was that what she had sensed?

She laid the pillow aside and pushed the comforter off the bed. It whispered to the floor, and Danzer turned to glance at it, his eyes lifting to hers before he turned away again. She looked at the rumpled sheets and wondered if he'd even bothered to tuck them in. Men. They were twice as helpless as women. Look at her, she could track, trap and shoot, as well as cook and keep a house. She could certainly make a decent bed. She stripped the old sheets away and left them in a crumpled heap at her feet, then shook out the clean ones. She did the bottom first, stretching way across the bed to make a neat pleat in the far corner. Next, she folded down the top sheet, went through the process of making the corners at the head of the bed and tucked in the sides. She folded the top sheet up and reached for the blanket, her hand colliding with Danzer's. He clicked the razor off, his brown eyes snagging hers. Laney felt a shock surge up her arm through her fingertips.

"Let me help you," he said quietly, and she nodded, catching her breath. He laid down the razor, and they slowly straightened, each taking a corner of the airy spread. He smiled at her across the ivory comforter, and her body tingled as if he'd actually touched her. They carried the down-filled cover over the bed and released it. It floated down and settled. Laney reached to straighten it, and Danzer hurried to help her, wincing at the sudden movement.

"What's wrong?" she asked quickly, her smooth brow furrowing. He stiffly lifted a hand to the back of his neck.

"Guess I'm just a marshmallow," he said. "Sleeping on the ground and living off the land is hard work, but I didn't expect to be this sore." He gave her a limp smile. "If you want to know the truth, skinning out that bear just about did me in."

She grinned at him. "Not as easy as it sounds, is it?"

"Nope, and it sounds hard enough. I can't believe you do that sort of thing for a living."

She laughed. "Well, I do. And because I do, I know just what your problem is. Why don't you lie down here, and I'll give you a good back rub."

He stared at her, his eyes very direct and probing. She wondered what on earth she was doing, and she knew she could retract that invitation without repercussion, but she didn't. She lifted her chin, surprised at how level she could keep her gaze, and he tilted his head to the side in reply, the corner of his mouth screwing upward, the corresponding brow arching. He leaned into the bed on one knee, slowly bent at the waist and let himself down across it, hands first. He folded his arms beneath his chin and rolled his eyes up at her.

"Okay, Dr. Scott, practice your healing art."

Laney slipped her shoes off and crawled onto the bed on her hands and knees, her bottom lip caught between her teeth. She sat back on her heels and stared down at his bare torso. The muscles ridged nicely along the slopes of his shoulders and flattened into smooth, curved blades that moved beneath the tanned skin. A clean indentation ran down the center of his back in a strong, straight line, the muscles swelling on either side to hard, thick planes and flattening at the base before the rise of his buttocks. Laney filled her lungs and reached out with trembling fingers to press on the small of his back, her thumbs wedged against his spinal column. His skin was cool but heated quickly as she pushed her hands over it.

"Ah. There," he said, his voice muffled by the comforter. She worked the tensed muscles, kneading, rubbing, squeezing until he sighed, the tension gone. She went on to his shoulders, working her thumbs beneath the blades, from the outside in and up to the taut column of his neck. "Wonderful," he muttered. "Glorious."

She smiled, her fingers making tiny circles that made his head bob from side to side. Her legs began to cramp, and she paused long enough to renegotiate her position, sitting instead of kneeling, her long legs thrust out across the bed, her feet hanging off the edge.

Danzer lifted his head, pushing up on his elbows, and his eyes automatically followed the graceful line of her legs. For a long moment he seemed frozen, stymied. Then, slowly he shifted over onto his side, his upper body weight balanced on one hand while the other reached out and covered her knee.

Her breath seized, and her heart abruptly doubled pace as he slid that hand up her leg, his body arching forward, his face suddenly inches away, his eyes wide and mesmerizing, his lips parting as they came to meet hers. She took his tongue into her mouth, her arms springing up to settle about his neck. He manipulated her mouth, his smooth chin thrusting against hers, his nostrils flaring against her cheek. Suddenly heat seared through her, flashing upward from the apex of her legs, striking through her abdomen and up into her chest, nipples hardening, gooseflesh sprouting on the back of her neck and along her spine. He spread his hand, forcing her legs apart, and she shuddered convulsively, abandoning his mouth as moist waves of heat rolled through her.

He took his hand away. His arms came up around her, one hand cupping the back of her head, the other hand positioning her face so that he could take her mouth again, driving his tongue into it, plundering deeply and thoroughly, until her fingers dug into his shoulders and she trembled, passion wracking her. He broke away, his mouth traveling across her cheek to her ear, and she gasped, eyelids shuttering up, then down again. He pushed her arms down and slid her sweater over them, tugging the cuffs over her hands, and tossed it away. His hands lifted to her hair and untied the string so it tumbled down about her shoulders, while his mouth tasted the soft underside of her jaw.

Laney placed her hands against his hard middle and slipped them upward over his chest. The tiny, crisp hairs parted for her fingers, tickling, teasing. He lifted his head, his eyes capturing hers, holding them, and she felt his hands at her waist, gently pulling her T-shirt free of her shorts. She held her breath, mesmerized, as ever so gently he peeled the shirt up and slipped it over her head and down her arms. She ook it from him and dropped it onto the bed. His hands kimmed up her arms and over her shoulders, then down until they found the closure of her bra. He dropped his mouth to the curve of her shoulder, nipping the sensitive lesh, and his fingers released the hook, moving to the traps, sliding them over her shoulders. She withdrew her arms, and this last barrier fell away.

His mouth traveled across her shoulder to the delicate ollow of her collarbone and downward, driving her head back. Her eyes closed as his hot, moist breath scalded a trail o the pinnacle of her swollen breast, and she sucked in her breath as he circled it with his tongue and moved on to the other, drawing the hard, dusky nub into his mouth. Laney ought her heart would burst through her chest and shater into a billion tiny pieces that would sparkle like stars in the charged air. He abandoned the breast, comforting it with his hand as his mouth seized the other. She laced her fingers in his hair, exulting in this new, exotic sensation, and his free hand splayed against her back, steadying her as he suckled. It was the oddest thing. It was her breast at which his mouth stroked and pulled, but she felt it in the pit of her stomach, a searing, liquid flame that licked upward and opened spaces in her she hadn't known existed, spaces that wanted, needed, filling. He tore away suddenly and pushed her down upon the bed, bringing his legs around until he could stretch out atop her.

"I thought of you," he said, levering himself up onto his elbows. "I thought of *this*. I tried not to, but every moment you were there in my mind, torturing me with the need to touch you, taste you." He let himself down very slowly, bare skin touching bare skin. His weight pressed her into the mattress, the light fur on his chest like silk on her breasts. "Tell me you want to make love to me," he whispered against her cheek. "*Ask* me to make love to you. God, Laney, say it. Say it!"

But she couldn't get the words out. They were staggering, enormous words, and as badly as she wanted to, sh
couldn't get them out. Why must anyone ask? Why did h
not just take what she was unable to freely give, yet unabl
to hold back? Didn't he understand that if he left her—*whe*
he left her—she didn't want to blame herself for letting thi
happen? It would be so much easier if she could blame hir
or an overwhelming passion or insanity, or anything. H
laid his forehead in the curve of her neck where it met he
shoulder, sighing. After a moment, he rolled away, fallin
face up beside her.

"Damn," he said. "Damn us both!"

She caught her breath and held it. He understood. Onl
too well, he understood. "I'm sorry," she whispered.

"We're both sorry," he said. "We both want it to hap
pen, but we're neither of us willing to take responsibility fo
it. A very adult pair, we are."

"I'm sorry," she whispered again, and he shifted onto hi
side, his arm sliding across her.

"Don't beat yourself up, baby. It's not worth it. Believ
me, I know." He pulled the side of the comforter up an
folded it over her.

She couldn't quite meet his eyes. "I guess you've know
lots of women, haven't you?" she asked timidly.

He said nothing for a long while, then lifted his hand t
her face and tilted her chin back, forcing her eyes.up. "No
so many," he said. "And none like you, not one." He kisse
the tip of her nose, and she lowered her gaze again, a smil
working across her mouth.

"What's so different about me?"

"I don't know," he said, his hand sliding down he
throat. "I wish I did. It's like...I'm out of my depth. I can'
quite figure out what to do with you."

She switched her eyes to his and held them there. "Mayb
that's how it's supposed to be," she said, swallowing be

cause her voice trembled. "I figure we've sort of got to work through this together, you know?"

He traced an imaginary line from the center of her forehead, between her eyes, and down her nose to her mouth. "You're pretty smart for a wood sprite," he said, and she smiled up at him.

"You're pretty special yourself, fly boy."

He kissed her, long and lingeringly, then growled into the hollow of her cheek and pushed himself away. "Get dressed, sweetheart, and run like hell before I change my mind."

He found her bra and handed it to her, then searched the covers for her T-shirt while she struggled into the bra under the corner of the blanket. She took it from him, thrust her arms through the sleeves and sat up, pulling it on. He held her sweater in his hand. She lifted her arm, and he slipped it on, gathering her hair out of the way as she searched for the second sleeve. She pulled the sweater together, and he spread her hair across her shoulders tenderly.

"Go," he ordered, whacking her on the bottom as she bounced off the bed. She laughed and hurried to the door, then turned to look at him. He stood with arms akimbo, his chest raising memories that hardened her nipples.

"The linens," she said, stepping forward and stooping to gather the crumpled sheets from the floor. "I've got to take them down." She stood with them in her arms.

"You can take my linens down anytime," he said, "or bring them up."

"Or slip between them?" she ventured boldly. A nervous grin split his face.

"That, too."

She dropped her gaze, feeling wanton and sexy and desired.

"We'll see," she said at last. "We'll just see."

"Maybe we will." His eyes seemed to promise that they would, then he looked away, his hands going to his hips.

Laney reached behind her and found the doorknob, turned it and opened the door. Stepping around it, behind it, she backed through, catching the knob again and slowly pulling it closed. She stood outside the door, her shoulder against it, his rumpled sheets in her arms, knowing he was on the other side thinking about her. What would it have been like to make love with him? Would she be happier? Would he? Would it bind him to her somehow? Suddenly she knew she wanted that. She didn't want him to go away from here without her, but how could she leave this place, providing he would even want her? And what would she do if he didn't? How would she bear it?

Oh, things had been so simple once. But that simple life was gone. It had vanished the day Danzer Wilson had appeared, and she wondered if it would ever come again—or if she even wanted it to.

Chapter Eight

Laney watched as the plane lifted gracefully into the sky, its pontoons and retracted landing gear trailing sparkling droplets of water. She felt a sudden longing to go with it, to fly free of this valley and the confusion that plagued her, but the next moment guilt replaced the longing and she turned away, pushing thoughts of Danzer and escape to the back of her mind. The valley was hers again. Danzer and Weir and his party were gone. For a few hours at least, everything was as it had been. Or so she told herself.

An abrupt sharpening of her senses occurred. Laney stopped halfway between the lakeshore and the house. Silence beyond the gentle rustling of pine needles surrounded her. Her skin prickled, the air charged with a faint new presence. The scents of pine and musk and water and fish and leather and human habitation swamped her, a rich blend that intoxicated the nose. Leather. Laney turned in a slow, tight circle, her eyes skimming the treeline, a smile softening her lips. There, to the west, Crater waited, decked out in his fringed and beaded buckskins, bow in hand, his long white hair spread across his thin, rounded shoulders. She lifted a hand to shade her eyes and started casually toward him.

He fitted an arrow into the arc of the bow and held it, waiting. Suddenly he let it fly, pointing the arrow high into the sky. Laney halted, watching with bated breath the glistening flight of the feathered tail. It reached apex and smoothly curved. An instant later, she knew it was headed straight for her. Panic erupted and promptly dissipated. Crater would not hurt her. He did nothing without reason. She stood her ground. The arrow struck not ten inches from her left foot. She stared, then slowly stooped to pick it up from the dirt. The shaft had snapped and was held by a splintered strip of bent wood. The arrow, carefully notched, tipped with shaved rock and painted with vibrant designs, was ruined. She returned it to Crater, whose folded hands rested against the tip of his bow.

"Broken," he said, failing to take it from her hand, "but not severed. As I thought."

He was sad. Laney felt it like a deep, cold fissure inside. "I don't understand," she told him. "Were you divining?"

He nodded, his beard whispering against the buckskin he wore and the ceremonial feathers tied into his hair by narrow thongs of soft, beaded leather. "It come to me in a dream," he said, "and I knew I had to show ya." Laney stared at the broken arrow, some part of her growing still and flat. "The land is the tip," he went on, "and you're the tail. You're connected, you and the land, but broken. You'll always be connected, but you'll never be the same. Like that arrow, you'll never be one with the tip again."

Tears filled her eyes. "I don't want this, Crater."

He stared into the treetops, eyes seeing not needles and clouds but visions, real and imagined. "It's a different time, Mountain Child. What was right for me in my time is wrong for you in yours. Land's got to survive, Laney, in the here and now. Men like me, we didn't make it happen. There's a new way now, and them that love this place and know what it's about are charged with protectin' it. Don't forget that, girl o' my heart, and don't forget me.''

Laney threw her arms around him and felt his thin, tough frame tremble. "How could I forget you?'' she whispered. "You're my father and my brother, my priest and my friend.''

He straightened and dried his eyes on his sleeve. "Aye,'' he said, "and all that changes when you take a man to your heart. Love becomes your religion, and you, your own priest, and father and brother give you away to that love rather than be pushed aside by it, and he becomes your dearest friend, as he should.'' He sighed deeply. "I'm a man out of time, Laney. It's me what don't belong. You're in the right, girl, right place and right time, right frame of mind. I'll be goin'.''

"Wait.'' She placed a hand upon his arm. He halted, and she offered the arrow, but he shook his head.

"You keep it,'' he said, and reaching up he stripped the thong and the white tipped eagle feather from his hair. "And wear this for a reminder, not of me, but of who and what you are.''

She took the feather and, tucking the arrow in the band of her jeans, tied it to a tress of her hair. The white tip tickled her throat and the thong felt heavy and strong. "Father of my spirit,'' she said in solemn parody of a game they'd played in her childhood, "live long and happy.''

"That I've done already,'' he replied softly, his callused, wrinkled hand skimming her cheek. "And I want no part of this new age. I'll keep to my mountain and live out my dreams, then I'll sing my song and let the earth take me as I should, alone and proud. We die alone, Laney, but we weren't meant to live alone. I had you, but now don't you be alone, child. Life's not meant for that. If I've learned anything, it's that life ain't meant for that.''

He ducked his head and moved away, a ghost from the past haunting the forest with his love of the land. Laney stood straight and proud, an old door closing within her, new ones opening, until he vanished into the shadows. She took the arrow in her hand and turned back, halting only steps later to take her measure of the valley again. She knew the truth of it then. The valley hadn't changed. The mountains, the forest, the river, the lake, each was as it had always been. Even the big sky and the yellow orb of the sun were as they had been for time immemorial. She had changed. Time had fulfilled itself in her, and because she knew she had changed, she was free—of the mountain, of the valley, of old and treasured and immature loves. She lifted her face and smiled, at war with herself no longer, and walked purposefully toward the lodge.

It was dusk by the time the plane cleared the eastern peak and the blanket of blue water spread before them. Danzer felt a pang of fondness as the clearing and the lodge loomed across his horizon. He would hate never to return to this place, never to see it again. Hiram stepped from behind the house, shirtless, his rugged torso glistening with perspiration. Danzer grinned to himself. Fall was all but upon them, winter quick behind it, and he suspected that as the first snowfall drew nearer, that woodpile looked smaller and smaller to his friend. He made himself a silent pledge to double his daily quota and turned his attention at once to the lake coming up to meet him.

The landing was smooth and short, and Danzer knew he had improved considerably from that first heart-stopping attempt weeks earlier. Somehow the real thing was never like practice, he mused, and for reasons he couldn't begin to name, Laney popped into mind. Had all the others been practice and only Laney the real thing? he wondered. Or had he been isolated in these mountains too long?

He cruised up to the pier and cut the engines. She was there, smiling at him, a feather in her long, thick hair. It wasn't the isolation of the valley that made her so incredibly beautiful to him, that made his loins stir at the sight of her. He had a sudden inclination to let go, to give up and simply allow himself to love her, but the strength of that emotion was frightening, overwhelming, and he was only now breaking away from a place not his. This was a special place, a place to which he wanted to return time and again, but this was not *his* place. It was Hi's place and to a lesser extent Lillian's—and Laney's. The idea made him sad, irritable, and he pushed it away, smiling suddenly as he stepped out onto the wharf. Her eyes were gentle, peaceful, but that one look was all the greeting he got as his passengers followed him ashore. He made the introductions.

"Laney, this is Anthony Fernald and Bill Bernard."

"Gentlemen." She offered her hand to first one and then the other. "I'm your guide, Laney Scott. Welcome to our valley."

The anger came unexpectedly, sharp, hot, deep. He had known, intellectually, that the moment was coming. Laney was, as he'd once pointed out, a competent professional. The idea was neither difficult to believe nor hard to imagine; yet, he found himself unable to accept the notion that she was actually going to trek into the wilderness, alone and unchaperoned, with two strange men!

Fernald and Bernard smiled and nodded at Laney. They were law partners in practice in Green Bay, Wisconsin. They *looked* like fish sellers. Fernald was slight and balding. Strings of colorless hair were combed over a patch of his ruddy scalp. He wore an expensive jogging suit and glasses thick as bricks. Bernard, in safari shorts, knee socks and sweatshirt, had thick, unruly red hair that stuck out in all directions and a face so freckled it was hard to tell where one brown spot left off and another began. Both were friendly in a bombastic way, and neither seemed unruffled at the prospect of a female guide. They seemed, in fact, completely harmless. Why, then, did the idea of the two of them being out there with Laney make Danzer feel like hitting something?

He managed to control himself until Laney and her charges left for the lodge. He even hurried their departure by volunteering to bring in their gear himself. As soon as they started down the pier toward shore, he secured the plane and opened the cargo hold. He was pulling bags and cases out onto the pier and muttering to himself about women and lawyers and stubbornness when a hand fell upon his shoulder and nearly sent him crashing into the water.

"Hiram!"

The older man clucked his tongue. "What's wrong with you, boy? You're jumpy as a salmon swimming upstream."

Danzer pulled a deep breath and calmed himself. "You startled me, that's all."

"Huh. That's funny. You're not the sort to startle easy. I think maybe you got something on your mind."

Danzer turned away determinedly, his jaw set against a tirade of words even he knew to be unfair.

"Nothing on my mind a good meal won't resolve."

He closed the cargo hold and began gathering straps and handles. Hiram automatically lent a hand.

"Well, if you don't want to talk," he said, "you don't want to talk."

"Nothing to talk about," Danzer muttered, hauling bags and bundles forward. "What've they got in here, a law library?"

"Oh, you never can tell," Hiram replied. "I ain't never surprised at nothin' these tenderfoots do. Neither is Laney. She's seen some shockers, that gal. Not a damned pack between 'em, I see. No, sir, no need to worry about our Laney. She can handle herself with even the looniest of tunes."

Danzer gritted his teeth. "Who said I was worried about Laney?"

Hiram just laughed. "Son, I wish you could see the look on your face sometimes."

They reached shore and dropped their burdens, taking a breather. "Am I that transparent?" Dan asked. Hiram rubbed his nose.

"No more than she is."

Dan looked off across the water, choosing his words.

"Doesn't it ever occur to you that she could be in more danger from these hunters than the mountain?"

"Yep. But what you don't understand is that these hunters are in more danger from Laney than anything they're likely to come across out there."

Danzer didn't know quite how to take that, and he wasn't really ready to concede the point. He knew Laney was capable. He knew she'd been doing this sort of thing for a long time. He knew Hi and Lil loved and treasured her. But he just couldn't quite accept it, and he couldn't understand how Hi and Lil could accept it. What if something happened out there? What if that pair of goons decided to take advantage of her? He didn't like her going out alone with them. He told himself it would be the same with any woman, but he knew it wasn't true, and that knowledge stuck in his craw like a bone. He just didn't know what to do about it.

"Sending her out there," he said at last, "alone, with a couple of strange men just doesn't seem *proper* to me."

Hi grinned and shouldered a brown leather clothing bag. "You just try to keep her from goin'," he said, and Danzer shot out a disgusted sigh.

"I know."

"'Course," Hi went on, threading his arm through the straps of a pair of matching bags, "you could always go along and see for yourself."

He hoisted the bags and moved away. Danzer watched his awkward waddle for a moment. The thought of spending several more nights on that mountainside was not inviting. Roughing it was something he was glad he'd done, something he was prepared to do again once or twice a year, tops, but the thought of doing so twice in the same week seemed worse than folly. On the other hand... No. He wasn't going to do it. It wasn't his problem. Let her do as she damned well pleased. He wasn't going to torture himself with cold, sleepless nights, days of exhaustion and meals with more grit than he had. He wasn't going to do it. Period. Maybe.

He felt like throttling himself, but what could he do? It hadn't been *that* bad, after all. He'd enjoyed himself well enough last time out. And it would be fun to see Laney in action. Maybe he would go. All right, he would definitely go. What difference did it make whether he lost sleep out there on the mountain or back here in the lodge? And why hadn't he stayed in Chicago where he was simply miserable? he wanted to know. Growling to himself, he scooped up the remainder of the baggage in one fierce hug.

"God, I hate bears!" he muttered.

He managed to get the mess of baggage into Lillian's kitchen. There Fernald and Bernard took over, moving the gear into the living room under Laney's direction. She had them lay it all out and open every piece. Hi sat at the dining room table, sipped coffee and chuckled to himself, unruffled by the ridiculous array of gadgets, gizmos and junk. Danzer could only shake his head.

Where in the wilderness, he wondered, did these idiots expect to plug in hair dryers, and why would they want them to begin with? But hair dryers were no more ludicrous than calculators, travel irons and food scales. (Bernard confessed he was watching his weight.) They'd even brought along a collection of magazines and books. Apparently they didn't expect to spend a single moment unentertained. And they had enough ammunition, had it been the right sort, to decimate the entire black bear population of the North American continent, not to mention a couple of other species.

Danzer knew he was going along. These two were certifiable, and he didn't intend to let sweet, delicious Laney cope with them all on her own for the next five days, no matter what Hiram Scott had to say about it. He picked his moment with care, waiting to broach the subject with Laney after dinner when she went out to the shed to get packs and other gear.

For some reason, he was as nervous as a pimply adolescent trying to swing his first date with the class beauty. He actually had to clear his throat, twice, before he could bring himself to speak.

"Listen, I was thinking." He paused to hold the flashlight steady while she unlocked the door.

"You taking a cold, Danzer?" she asked absently, fitting the key into the lock.

"Uh, no. I'm fine. I just had a little...um, catch in my throat. It's okay. Anyway, I was thinking."

"You said that already," she pointed out lightly, pocketing the key. She pulled the door open and walked in. Danzer followed, aiming the flashlight beam. She struck a match and lit a kerosene lamp that hung on the wall. He clicked off the light, staring about him at the clutter as she began moving about the cramped interior, slipping between tables and overturned canoes, taking things from the shelves in the rear and pegs along the wall.

"Well, what I was thinking," he went on, "is that I'd like to go along with you and, um, the guys."

She stopped, her hands filled with a first-aid kit, a sleeping bag under her arm. "Why, Danzer!" she exclaimed. "I'm surprised at you."

He shifted uncomfortably. "Sur-surprised? Why? What's surprising? I mean, that's what I came here for."

"Yes, of course, but I didn't think you'd want to go out again so soon."

He had to swallow. "Well, sure. Why not? Unless you don't want me along."

She laughed outright. "No, you can come along. I'll be glad to have you along. Just remember that this was your idea. All right?" She laid aside the articles she was holding and walked toward him, squeezing between the canoes again. His heart was beating whump-whump-whump, and he felt like a scared rabbit. Smiling, she approached and lifted herself up on tiptoe to place a chaste, delicate kiss on his rough cheek. "You're sure you want to do this?" she asked pointedly, and he nodded, itching to take her in his arms but reluctant to do so.

"Sure."

"Okay." She slipped away and went back to collecting her gear, occasionally sending him a smile over her shoulder.

This wasn't so tough, after all, he decided. This might even be fun. God knew Hi wasn't the most cheerful companion after a hard night on a cold mountain, and Fernald and Bernard, while not ideal companions, were less irritating than Weir and his bunch. Laney wouldn't drive them as hard as Hi. She *couldn't* drive them as hard as Hi, not lovely, feminine Laney. He got a picture of her beside a crackling campfire, the sky full of diamonds, the Two Stooges snoring in their blankets. Merciful heaven, what was he thinking? It shouldn't be that way. It couldn't be that way. Laney was not the sort of woman a man played with, and he was not the sort of man to tie himself down, not when he'd just freed himself, not now.

He told himself to let it be, to beg off. Laney had been doing this sort of thing for a long time now. She was in no danger. Fernald and Bernard were no threat. Why then couldn't he shake this feeling that he'd regret it if he let her go out there without him? Maybe he'd wake up in the morning and that feeling would be gone. And maybe she'd lose her appeal overnight. And maybe he should have his head examined. And maybe it was already too late for that.

They fell out at first daylight. Laney was cheerful, calm, organized. She cooked them a first-rate breakfast all by herself and left the three men to clean up while she made a final check of their gear. To Danzer's surprise, Hi and Lillian slept in. According to Laney that was standard procedure. When Dan and the other two joined her outside, she had already strapped on her pack, and theirs were lined up in strict order. Dan lifted and shrugged into his. Fernald looked like he was going to collapse under his, but the look on his thin face was grim determination. When all three were strapped up she took command, literally.

"All right, listen up," she ordered, sounding for all her worth like a drill sergeant. "Now these are the facts: I'm in charge. I'm the expert. I'll make the decisions. You will do as I say when I say. Anybody who doesn't like that arrangement can unbuckle and stay right here, but once we're on the trail, you'll do what I tell you to or you're likely to end up hurt. Is that perfectly clear?"

"Absolutely."

"Yes. Yes, indeed."

Fernald and Bernard were only too eager to agree. They acted, in fact, as if they wouldn't want it any other way.

Danzer, on the other hand, felt a perverse sense of rebellion—and she knew it. She brought both hands to her hips and leveled an implacable stare at him.

"Danzer?"

He blanched, shrugged, finally forced a nod. "Uh, yeah, sure. I . . . understand."

She studied him doubtfully for several seconds, then strolled forward and struck a stance just inches in front of him.

"Danzer," she muttered, "are you sure about this? I can't have you undermining my authority out there, and if you can't accept that . . ."

"I said, I understand!" he hissed at her, and she backed off.

"All right. Okay. As long as it's clear."

"Crystal clear!" he said through his teeth. Creeps, hadn't he been through enough over this already? He wasn't going to be any trouble. Trouble is what he was trying to prevent. Wasn't it?

She inclined her head and brought up both hands. "Don't get touchy."

Danzer closed his eyes, struggling for control. "Who," he said at last, "is touchy? I just want to go. I'm ready to go. Can we go now? *Please.*"

She raised a brow at him, turned on her heel and strode off, Fernald and Bernard hot on her trail. Danzer rolled his eyes and reluctantly brought up the rear, telling himself it was going to be all right. They were all adults. He'd survived Hi and the Weir gang; he could survive Laney and the Two Stooges. Everything was fine, wonderful. They were going to have a great time. Chances were Baldy and Red wouldn't even sight a bear, let alone actually kill one, and if they did—well, heck, he was a veteran, wasn't he? What could possibly go wrong?

Everything.

Bernard fell that very first afternoon. Danzer decided he hated climbing, especially because now that he'd chalked up a little experience he got to be last, which meant that when Bernard fell, he fell *on* Danzer. It couldn't have been frail, anemic Fernald. Oh, no. It had to be fat, clumsy Bernard. And his aim was perfect. One moment Danzer was looking up, watching Bernard's painful, trembling progress, and the next he saw that huge pack and those pudgy arms and legs falling toward him. The next thing he knew, he was flat on his back, the air knocked out of his lungs, an unbelievable pressure on his chest, and blue sky swimming overhead.

Miraculously neither of them were hurt. Bernard looked about ready to cry, but he was in better shape than Danzer, who gasped for air for five minutes before the first clear, painless breath filled his lungs again. Laney came down and listened to his chest, making certain that he hadn't punctured a lung. He wouldn't have been at all surprised if he'd broken half his ribs, but everything seemed intact. They waited a few minutes, with Fernald calling down to ask if everything was all right every thirty seconds, then Bern and Laney went up together. Danzer was amazed when the chubby redhead actually made it to the top, and Bernard himself was thrilled. He was some macho dude, according to Fernald, and it was clear Bernard's stock had gone up about 200 percent. They'd be telling this story for months, maybe years. Meanwhile, Danzer was hoping he could move come morning. He looked forward to a night among the rocks less and less.

They made camp early that evening, and much to Danzer's surprise, Laney brought out a tube of liniment to massage into his battered muscles. She even did the honors, after tending Bernard. Danzer gritted his teeth and tried not to think about the last time she'd given him a rubdown, but it was impossible not to conjure up those images of her lying beneath him, partially naked and trembling for his touch. To make matters worse, the fantasies did not leave when she did. They stayed to lurk at the back of his mind, torturing him.

The fire crackled just as he'd imagined it would, and when it got dark enough, the stars actually began to sparkle. He watched Laney as she moved about the camp, preparing their meal, advising her two charges on various matters to do with the next day's trek. Dinner was passable, there being few ways to ruin or improve canned hash, but Danzer couldn't focus on food. His mind was filled with Laney Scott, and he needed to do something about that. He needed to touch her, to hold her against him. Just that much would be enough, or so he told himself.

Laney assigned the task of cleaning up to Fernald, gave a few brisk instructions, and walked away. Danzer watched her go, fighting with himself about following her. He'd followed her once before. The memory assailed him, enveloped him. He got up and went after her, thinking that there were more things you just couldn't do anything about, some desires you just couldn't ignore. He'd think about it later. It was more important just then to stop the torment, to satisfy that greed in him for her. He never thought for even a moment that she would refuse him. How could she? Hadn't her own desire driven her to him twice now?

He'd reconciled himself to whatever the consequences might be the very moment he'd risen to follow her. They were hardly out of earshot of the camp when he reached for her, expecting her to come willingly into his arms. He wasn't prepared for the rigid resistance, the blazing glare. This was Laney, his Laney, the woman who trembled when he touched her, the woman who now looked like she was going to whip the hide off him.

"What the hell do you think you're doing?" she barked. He blinked at her, hands turned palms-up in confusion.

"I wanted . . . to talk to you." It sounded lame to his own ears, but suddenly he felt certain that it was unfair of her not to act as he'd expected. "You know damn well what I want," he said.

She stared at him. "Have you lost your mind?"

It was not at all what he'd expected her to say, not at all what he wanted to hear.

"Laney, I thought that we . . ."

"You thought? You thought? Danzer, you *haven't* thought at all!" she insisted hotly. "For Pete's sake, Danzer!"

He was dumbfounded. All he could think to do was pull her into his arms, but she did not come warmly. Instead, she was stiff and cold and unyielding.

"Stop it!" she ordered, turning her head away. "I can't have this, Dan."

His mouth fell open, and for the first time she seemed to sense that he was truly puzzled.

"Oh, Dan." She sighed, visibly relaxing, and stepped out of his embrace. "Please, Dan, look at this from my perspective. I've got Tweedledum and Tweedledee out there thinking they're Daniel Boone and Robinson Crusoe. In any other situation they'd be perfectly harmless, but out here there's real danger, and I can't have you undermining my authority. Just let one of those idiots get it into his head that he can ignore me or that an order is merely advice, and we've got a disaster on our hands. I have to maintain control. I thought you understood that."

It did, unfortunately, have a certain logic to it, but if he couldn't even touch her, how was he supposed to deal with this need, this compulsion? The days ahead suddenly appeared bleaker than he could have imagined. She couldn't mean this, and even if she did, she couldn't expect it to work. Could she?

"I'm not trying to challenge you, honey," he began, bu
she threw up her arms in disgust.

"Danzer, *honey* is not here!" she told him. "I left he
back at the lodge with sweetie, baby and sugar lips. Are yo
getting my message?"

"Hell, yes! I got it. Sheesh! Can't a guy even be *nice* t
you? I mean, is it a challenge to your supreme authority t
make nice?"

She folded her arms and stared at him. "No," she said
"But I've seen nice from you, and I've seen that look i
your eye. That look is not *nice*. It's why-the-hell-not? It'
just-let-go. It's lousy timing, is what it is! And I cannot af
ford that kind of major distraction!"

Major distraction? He liked the sound of *that*.

"Me?" he said, affecting innocence. "A distractio
maybe, but a major distraction? Not me."

The anger went out of her eyes and amusement entere
them. He felt a perverse pride in that.

"Yes, you!" she declared, giving him a playful push
"Back to camp now. Go on. And don't think I'm going t
change my mind about this."

"Won't you?" he asked softly, and she shook her head
solemn again.

"No, Dan, I won't. I can't, and if you feel anything fo
me at all, you'll do as I ask."

How was a guy supposed to argue with that? He knew
unhappily, that his desire wasn't going to be satisfied ou
here. He opted for putting on the best face that he could.

"You're the boss."

"By Jove, I think you've got it."

"Yes, ma'am. You can count on me, ma'am." He
snapped her a salute and winked, walking backward. "Bu
just in case you find yourself overcome with passion at some
point, remember I'm the tall one."

She contained a smile. "The bruised one is more like it."

"Ha-ha. Very funny. Say, have I told you you're very beautiful by firelight?"

Her hand shot out in a straight line, pointing. "Go, Dan. *Now.*"

"This isn't going to work," he said, walking sideways.

"You just keep your distance from now on," she told him. "I mean it, Dan. I don't want trouble with you."

"It wasn't what I had in mind, either," he assured her.

She glared and locked her arms, then whirled and strode away in the opposite direction. Danzer shook his head, partly amused, partly dismayed. She couldn't be serious. Who was to know what went on between them in private? What business was it of Boone and Crusoe, anyway? She picked a wonderful time to decide she couldn't afford any intimacy with him. She'd change her mind, though. He wasn't the only one who craved the kind of fire they could make together. She wanted him. She couldn't deny that. She couldn't treat him like he was some ordinary fellow. She couldn't keep him on a par with Bernard and Fernald. She would definitely change her mind. It was only a matter of time.

She didn't change her mind. For four perfectly miserable days and four even worse nights, she treated him like the third Stooge. *Do this Danzer. Now. Do that Danzer. Immediately. And above all else keep your hands to yourself.* He was homicidal by the time they found their bear and turned homeward. Thank God they decided not to shoot it. He didn't think he could've gone through that again. He didn't think Bernard could go through with it, and he knew Fernald would have been puking his guts out before the first cut was made. Laney didn't argue when Fernald hesitated. No one argued. She tried to make the situation a little more palatable by saying the bear wasn't legal game anyway, though Danzer knew better and suspected the firm of Fernald and Bernard did, too. But then by that time Laney could've said the moon was made of green cheese, and those two idiots would have been ready to rewrite the textbooks.

As far as they were concerned, Laney Scott was the greatest thing ever to come down the pike. She was smart, confident, dependable, tough and "the best-looking dad-burned guide in the whole damn Rocky Mountains." The longer they were out, the more Bernard affected this imaginary mountain-man lingo. Dan wanted to strangle him and Fernald with his bare hands, both of them. Along about the middle of the third day, he'd started praying they'd both fall off a cliff. He'd even tried to mentally exhort the bear to come and eat them, but that bear had more sense than he'd counted on. Shoot, it had more sense than *he* did.

There could be no doubt that Laney Scott knew her stuff, though. There could be even less doubt that she meant what she said and said what she meant, and it didn't trouble Dan so much that he couldn't touch her as it troubled him that he was so blasted *troubled* that he couldn't touch her. It was five days of pure hell made worse by the sure knowledge that Fernald and Bernard were thoroughly smitten by, wholly in awe of, and even now embellishing imaginative personal tales about their stubborn, capable, incredibly beautiful guide. Dan wanted to tell those two losers in no uncertain terms that *he*—and only he—had had her in his bed, and if either one of them so much as laid a soft white hand on her, he'd have it skinned and dressed out in a quarter of an hour.

He did not, of course, so much as open his mouth. If he had, he had no doubt that she would have closed it for him even if she'd had to do it with a rock. There is proof, he could have noted for posterity, that agony of spirit can addle the mind and still leave one perfectly able to reason. He promised himself he would live through this without acting like a complete fool, and to his credit, he did just that.

On the morning they returned to the lodge, he managed to be pleasant and polite to everyone. Out of habit, or perhaps out of fear of what would happen if he relaxed his guard, he steered clear of Laney. He made it through breakfast and unpacking and a long, hot shower and even a nap before the time came to fly his two fares back to Great Falls where he'd met them.

Time was of the essence, however. A third hunting party was waiting in Helena, and while the distances to be covered were comparatively short, so was the afternoon, and he didn't want to be caught flying over these mountain peaks after dark. He was tired and irritable, and didn't trust his own emotional state at the moment.

In the mountains Laney had been right, of course. He could admit that now, even feel relieved that he had been foiled in his determination to have her and be damned. Such a powerful feeling as he'd felt had to have been more than desire. He feared it might have been love. And if she had given in to him on the hunt, she would have known it. It was enough to scare the blood right out of his veins, enough to make him feel like the greatest heel alive—since he didn't intend to let himself fall in love.

Everyone was there on the dock that afternoon: Hi, Lil and most importantly, Laney. Skinny little Fernald and his fat, blustering partner were stowing their copious luggage. General goodbyes had been said, and the Scotts, with the exception of Laney, had backed away in anticipation of an imminent takeoff. Fernald and Bernard finished with their task and turned for a final farewell. Danzer secured the cargo compartment and turned also. It was then that she did it. She stepped forward, as calm as the lake in morning, lifted both arms and draped them about his neck, pressed herself against him, and brought her mouth down hard over his.

Danzer was stunned, breathless, thrilled, appalled. It was as public a statement as if she'd hired a skywriter and emblazoned it across the sky.

By the time she finished that kiss, and it did take considerable minutes, every person present knew exactly how she felt about him. Even Danzer knew, and it was almost more than he could cope with after days of stone cold denial. He put his arms around her and joined warmly in the kiss. In truth, he never thought to do otherwise. But neither could he stop the look of shock on his face afterward or the growling replies he made to Fernald and Bernard's good-natured ribbing—or the swell of pride that puffed out his chest and the white hot desire that shot through his body and hardened painfully in his groin.

Somehow, he got in the plane, went through his checklist and got them into the air. But long before he cleared that first white crest, he knew he'd made a terrible mess of things. He was the one who had said, more or less, that someone would have to take responsibility before they could make love. When he'd gone to her, she'd naturally concluded that he was that someone, and by kissing him like that in front of her parents, she'd pretty much declared her feelings. Dear God, what had he gotten himself into?

Love was not in the careful plans he'd made. It was not one of the dreams with which he'd set out to indulge himself. It was impossible, impractical, unworkable, unrealistic. And there it was, staring him in the face, whirling about his head. What was he going to say to that girl when he got back? How was he going to act? What was he going to do? He had some decisions to make, and never had he felt so inadequate to the task, so perplexed, so swamped...so scared.

Some vacation this had turned out to be. Some simplification. Indulge yourself, Danzer! You deserve it! Go ahead, boy! Just don't break that sweet woman's heart, whatever you do. Whatever the hell you do, don't hurt her—if you can help it.

Chapter Nine

Laney pulled her coat together and drew her knees up against her chest. She shivered inside the cocoon of nylon and down. The second week of September had ended on a mild day that had faded into a chilly night, and still Danzer had not returned. She didn't understand, and she feared she never would. She bowed her head against her knees and felt the crisp air on the nape of her neck where her thick hair parted and swung forward. In her mind she felt his hand cover the spot and warm it. A sensation like hot liquid flowed through her, and for the hundredth time in the past two days, tears filled her eyes.

She heard footsteps across hard-packed ground, and she knew from the cadence that it was her father coming to check on her. Quickly she lifted her head and dried the tears, composing her face with studied serenity, not that she expected to fool him. Her parents both knew that she was in very real pain and had been since they'd received word of the cancellation of the last Helena party. A radio operator at the airport had relayed the message: their party of two had been called back to Oklahoma due to a personal emergency, and their pilot would contact them later about resuming the schedule. There had been no further explanation, and, after more than forty-eight hours, no further word. She wondered if he would ever return. In the blackest moments when she felt certain she would never see him again, she even imagined that he had crashed and was at that very moment lying dead upon some remote mountainside. But that was the work of panic and fear and uncertainty, all emotions relatively unfamiliar to her. In her calmer moments, she knew it was foolishness.

Hiram came walking up through the trees, making plenty of noise, and called out to her. She rose from the stump where she had been sitting and stepped out into the small clearing so he could discern her silhouette from the dark shapes of the trees around her. He came puffing up, his shirt sleeves dark against the shiny orange of his nylon vest.

"Your mother's worried about you, gal. Can't you come back to the house and set her mind at ease?"

Laney nodded and stepped forward, slipping her arm through his. "Sure, Dad. It's getting cold anyway."

He turned, and together they strolled down the slope. At the edge of the trees they paused by silent consensus and gazed down on their home.

"Beautiful, isn't it?" he observed, and Laney hugged his arm tightly.

"I've always thought it was a special place," she said. "I always felt safe and insulated here and especially privileged. It was as if nothing that happened outside mattered. We made our own reality, in a way."

"And now the wide world has intruded in the form of a man," he stated simply. Laney sighed and studied the glow of the fire through the window of the great room.

"I think I knew on some level that it would happen on day," she said, "but I didn't want to face the possibility. guess you could say I didn't want to grow up because I knew the life I could make for myself wouldn't be what you and Mama have built."

"And it shouldn't be, Laney. You need to make your own way. Your mother and I have realized that right along. We always figured some fellow would come and take you away from this valley, or that you'd just choose to go on your own. We've been expecting it for a long time now, and I'll tell you the truth, Laney, I'm almost ready to go myself. It's a hard life out here, and I'm tired. Oh, I'll always want to come back. This place is part of me. But I want life to be easier, and I'm tired of sharing my home with strangers, dadgumit! I want to sit back and enjoy this place. I'm sick to death of babysittin' every greenhorn what fancies himself a hunter and has two nickels to rub together. I've earned that much. So have you."

She laid her head upon his shoulder, and after a moment they resumed their walk, heading west, that lighted window their guide. Laney let the question roll around in her head several times before she asked it.

"Do you suppose he'll come back?"

Hiram patted her hand. "I'd say yes, but then I'm prejudiced. Speaking strictly as your father, I just don't see how he could stay away from you."

"Guess he can," she muttered. "He's not here."

Hiram chuckled, matching his stride to hers. "Give him time, girl. Love can be a scary thing for a man. He doesn't always see it as this grand adventure you females do."

Laney stopped and pulled away a little, staring at her father. "Do I detect a note of confession here?"

He rubbed his raspy chin with his free hand. "A man sometimes thinks of love as a matter of obligation and responsibility, and those things can be a hindrance. Maybe he's got his mind set on achieving a certain ambition or a way of life, or maybe he doesn't know what he wants and figures he can't find out and be responsible to a woman, too." He shook his head, and she glimpsed a kind of faraway, remembering look about him. He shook it off and started to walk again, tugging at her arm.

"Were you scared to marry Mama?" she asked after a bit. He gave his head a slow, serious nod.

"I was scared to death."

"But everything's worked out fine," she protested lightly.

"I didn't know that then. When I got down to really thinking about it, I figured out I couldn't be happy in these mountains without her, and I knew if I couldn't be happy here I couldn't be happy anywhere. So, I tamped down the fear and went ahead with it."

"Have you ever regretted it?" she asked. He thought a moment.

"I've regretted making life so hard for her at times. I've regretted not putting her first in some decisions I've made. But, generally speaking, no, I haven't regretted lovin' or marryin' your mother, not a minute of it."

Laney stroked his strong arm and smiled and felt the clouds lifting a little. Hiram laughed and shook his head, and they went on home together in silence, comforted and encouraged.

It was the fourth day when the whine and chug of the airplane at last permeated the natural silence of the Scott's valley. Laney was in her room, oiling her treasured furniture, when the sound reached her. For a moment, she thought she was imagining the sound, but then her father's voice came booming up to her.

"Laney? *La-ney!* Come down!"

Danzer had come home! Dropping the oil rag, she ripped the bandanna from her head and hastily cleaned her oily

fingers with it. Frantic, she grabbed a comb, pulled it once
through her hair, snagging it, and tossed it aside, using her
hands instead to smooth and fluff her rich brown tresses as
she rushed from the room. She met her dad on the way up,
coming to get her.

"It's about time! Didn't you hear? That's Danzer! He's
come..."

She left him standing at the foot of the stairs and passed
her mother as she stepped out of the hallway, drying her
hands on her apron, an anxious look on her face. The sound
sputtered and drifted away as she tore through the kitchen.
When she pushed out into the soft September sunshine, only
the lapping and swishing of water was left to proclaim the
arrival.

Laney forced herself to slow down as she rounded the
corner of the house, but her heart leapt at the sight of the
familiar craft at the end of the pier, and there was Danzer,
wrapping the anchor rope securely about the post. He
straightened suddenly and turned. For a moment, her throat
closed up, shutting in words as well as breath. Then his hand
shot into the air, and he was moving with long, swift strides
down the pier toward shore. He was smiling. The air rushed
in, and she started forward, holding herself to a disciplined
jog. She drew up short, her heart hammering as if she'd run
miles.

"Laney!"

"You're back." She had a hard time keeping her voice
steady, but tried again. "We were worried. You were gone
so..."

He reached out and curled his hand beneath her chin,
stopping the words and tilting her head.

"I missed you," she said softly, and he stepped forward.
She came instantly into his arms, threw her own about him
and exulted in the feel of his mouth on hers. He hugged her
close and kissed her again, delving into her mouth with his

tongue, fitting her body to his with his hands, a small adjustment here, a bit of pressure there, until, satisfied, his arms closed about her again, a warm, strong cocoon. When he broke away a second time, it was to burrow into the wealth of her hair and find a tender place somewhere behind and below her ear to brush with his lips.

"I'm glad you're back," she said, the words compressed as a result of his embrace.

"You're lovely to come back to," he whispered, and Laney closed her eyes, holding this moment in time. She wouldn't let herself cry or be angry or be anything but happy.

He arched backward, lifting her feet from the ground, and she laughed aloud, feeling small and feminine and pretty. He set her down again, and his hands skimmed her head and face and shoulders. His eyes were crinkled at the outer corners and gleaming. She thought of asking him all those questions that had haunted her these past four days—why, where, with whom—but somehow it was enough just to have him here, to be greeted this way, to feel his hands moving, stroking, touching her in a dozen small, different ways.

"Gregory Princeton says hello."

"Who's Gregory Princeton?"

"You remember. The guy at the airport with the pretty wife."

Envy stabbed her. "Do you really think she's pretty?"

He grinned. "In a dainty, helpless way." She actually felt the beginnings of a pout, but before she could scold herself, he pulled her against him again. "You, on the other hand, are beautiful, resourceful and graceful."

She lifted her mouth to his, feeling the friction against her breasts and thighs. She held the kiss a long, lovely time, enjoying the effects of it in her body, the tightenings and openings, the pulsings and flowings. She knew equally delicious things were happening to him, and it pleased her, thrilled her, to be the cause of it. The judicious clearing of a throat put a sudden end to that private business.

They turned simultaneously, arm in arm, to see Hi and Lillian Scott in exactly the same posture, watching. Laney's eyes grew wide. Danzer's breath stopped and rushed out again. Lillian bowed her head, her hand going to her mouth, while Hiram stepped briskly forward, at a loss, it seemed, for something to do with his hands. He was grinning, though, and that made Laney relax.

"We got your message, Danzer. Thanks for that."

"Hi, I'm sorry we lost that last party..."

"Aw, no. Couldn't be helped. Gave us some time off." He shifted his weight. "Guess you needed a break, too."

Danzer lifted a hand to the back of his neck, the other at Laney's waist. "Well, it came at a good time, anyway. The plane developed an electrical problem on the flight down from Great Falls and it gave me time to do a little maintenance."

"No need to explain," Hiram said, reaching around to pat Danzer on the back. "You're back in plenty of time for the next transport. We did sort of expect you to radio in, though."

Danzer took a deep breath. "The, um, electrical problems were... Well, you know, it occurred to me I ought to have a portable radio. I can't be in the plane all the time, and you might need to reach me for something, and, well, I thought I'd look into that."

"Sure. You bet. Whatever you think. We could split the cost, you know."

"No, no." Danzer stepped back, bringing Laney over in front of him. He rested both hands on her shoulders. It was such a natural gesture, such a possessive one. She laid her head back against his chest. "We'd just have to settle up later, one way or another," he said. "I'll take care of it."

That wasn't exactly what she'd hoped to hear. His arrangement with her father would come to an end, of course, but she'd begun to think of him staying—or of going away with him. She looked at her parents, knowing they'd thought the same things, surprised a little at the way they were taking this. Did they really believe it could happen? Did they understand, really, that she was deeply, desperately in love? How could they when she didn't quite understand it herself?

Lillian insisted they all go in for cups of coffee and chunks of the nut-flavored pound cake she'd spent the morning making. It gave Danzer's homecoming a celebratory feeling and eased the few tensions. Laney knew her parents were trying to be deferential and that it was for Danzer's sake as well as hers. She was glad and—and worried that it wouldn't last, couldn't last. Such feelings were fragile and delicate. Like fine china, they could be broken by careless intent or rough handling.

Danzer, too, seemed to be taking care. He laughed and smiled and said all the right things at all the right times; yet Laney sensed an uncertainty, a temerity that seemed both baseless and understandable. One thing, though, she could not mistake, and that was the way he looked at her, hungrily, longingly, as if she was all that stood between him and starvation. She could feel that look on her skin and deeply within her body. It made her feel powerful and desired and utterly female. For the first time, she supposed she knew what that word *female* actually meant, and it had a frightening quality about it that both dismayed and thrilled her.

They wiled away the afternoon with the kind of shallow chatter and busyness that attends uncertainty. She found an odd patience though, in her empathy for him. She understood that uncertainty and trusted, hoped, it would pass. He had been drawn to her just as she had been drawn to him, helplessly, deeply, undeniably. He would come to the same conclusion that she had. He would understand, finally, that they had to be together. Wouldn't he?

By silent, mutual consent, they chose to behave as if he'd never left, their passionate greeting notwithstanding. Hi and Lillian made it easy for them, playing their roles with ease and nonchalance. They went through dinner in that mode and into the evening. Danzer played chess with Hiram and lost, then gave up the board to Laney, who concentrated doubly hard and managed to win. It was during that second game when she was so intent that he slipped out. She wasn't surprised somehow to look up and find him gone, but she found it suddenly difficult to sit there without him, wondering what he was doing, wondering if her parents were wondering. After several silent minutes, she couldn't stand it any longer. She got up and went out through the front door. It was something she hardly ever did, use that door. It seemed much more natural to walk through the dining area, hallway and kitchen, but not tonight.

She knew at once that he was there and scanned the surrounding vista, the house to her back. The night air was "crisp to breaking" as Crater would have said, and she shivered, saddened a bit at the passing of summer. Her eyes scanned the black shapes at the edge of the black night across the silver shadowed clearing where the tapered bole of the flagpole stood in sharp, inky relief. The spires of the pines spiked black against a midnight-blue sky strewn with white, gleaming pinpricks of light. The winking of the stars seemed the only movement. Laney waited, knowing her eyesight would adjust, her instincts sharpen. She kept her gaze slowly moving, sweeping the area once, twice. The third time she saw him, or rather his shape, his back against a tree trunk, one knee flexed and protruding. She smiled and started forward toward the black fringe of the forest.

She crossed the clearing, knowing well that he watched her, fearing that he preferred she leave him to his solitary musing. He stood away from the tree as she drew near, and she felt his eyes on her in a way she could not explain. It made her skin prickle, a sensation that had become familiar to her and welcome. She halted before him, saying nothing, open to all her senses might tell her, expectant. He stepped forward and lifted his hands to her shoulders. They felt heavy and warm and strong.

"Are you okay?" she asked softly.

"No," he said.

She pulled in a slow, deep breath, trying to forestall the sudden panic she felt. "Can... can I help?"

"No," he said again, then, "Yes," and finally, "Hell."

She didn't know what to say to that, what to think. Then something her father had said came back to her, and she looked up into Danzer's face, fastening her gaze on the gleam of his eyes.

"You stayed away because of me, didn't you?" He dropped his hands, saying nothing. He didn't have to. "There was never anything wrong with the plane, was there?"

"No."

"There was nothing wrong with the radio."

"Nothing."

"You're afraid of the way I feel about you."

He pushed a hand up into his hair. "Terrified," he admitted gruffly.

She fought the urge to grab onto him, to make him touch her, bind him to her. She lifted her chin, her heart throbbing painfully.

"Is it the way I feel about you or the way you feel about me?" she pressed. Several seconds passed, dragged, crept by.

"Both," he said at last, and fresh air flooded into her lungs. Yet, somehow she had known. And now he knew.

She clasped her hands together in an unconscious act of celebration.

"My father told me," she explained breathlessly. "It was the same with him for my mother, the very same." She heard his smile.

"Now why doesn't that reassure me?" he asked, but at the same time, his hands came out and claimed her. Pivoting, he turned her, so that her back was now to the tree. She sensed what was coming, and her body reacted accordingly.

"I don't know," she said, forgetting the question as he filled his hands with her breasts. She gasped, and her head fell back against the tree trunk, her eyelids snapping shut. He pressed against her, his hands at her breasts, his mouth taking hers. She felt a fierce, awesome joy in this passion, welcomed it, greeted it. She locked her arms around his waist and slipped her tongue into his mouth. He rewarded her with a sharp quickening of his breath and increased pressure from his hips, which she returned wantonly, carelessly. He wrapped his arms around her, and she felt her breasts flatten against his chest. The cracked back of the tree was rough against her spine, the air cool against her skin, his breath hot and quick against her cheek, his body hard, his mouth firm and moist and soft on the inside where her tongue teased and stroked. In the rightness of it all, she forgot the fears, the confusion, the questioning, the uncertainty. She forgot to wonder what he was thinking, feeling. She forgot to worry, to posit, to weigh, and simply gave herself up to desire, knowing instinctively that it was this that bound them, that brought them together time and again, and would do so until their hearts, each in its own way, decided what the future should hold for them.

Danzer poured himself a cup of complimentary coffee and sat down. He was beginning to dislike this airport wait ing room, which was silly—as was so much he'd done of late, like staying here in Helena those four lonely nights when what he'd wanted was to spend those nights with Laney. He'd accomplished nothing in all that time. He'd resolved nothing, concluded nothing, decided nothing. What was he to do? He couldn't stay away. He couldn't make himself stay away; yet he couldn't stay indefinitely. He had it in the back of his mind to promise her he would return in nine months. He'd know what he wanted then, and if they still felt the same way about each other... well, he'd cross that bridge when he came to it.

He looked at her now, in blue jeans and a gold turtleneck sweater worn beneath a brown corduroy jacket, her lazy gaze fastened on the rim of her cup, her legs stretched out before her, ankles crossed. She was a lovely woman, and not only that. She was a capable woman, too. That thought had occurred to him before, but a new one followed it: he admired her. She was perhaps the most confident, self-assured woman he'd ever known. Yes, he admired her. And he wanted her. So much so his body reacted to that desire even now.

He tugged his eyes away and concentrated his attention on his cup, telling himself to keep his mind off making love to her, no easy task considering the memories with which he had to contend. Last night. Last night she had met him stroke for stroke, need for need, and the shots had been his to call. He could have made love to her. He still remembered with tingling clarity the sound the zipper on her jeans had made when he'd separated it, but somehow he'd gritted his teeth and made himself stop, just as he'd done that day she'd come to his room and that evening on the mountain. He closed his eyes against the vision of her beneath him on his bed, naked from the waist up, mouth parted, hair spread across the coverlet, only to see it all the more clearly. He spilled his coffee.

"Dan!" She laughed and grabbed the paper napkins they'd brought from the concession with their doughnuts, mopping the warm brown liquid from his lap. He leapt up, proclaiming himself an idiot, mortified at the reaction her thoughtless touch had provoked. She laughed again, not the least put off. And he thought that if it were not for the possibility of being found in a compromising position right here in the airport courtesy room, he'd take her into his arms now, strip away the layers of clothing, fill his hands and mouth with her and satisfy this desire for them both—and then be obliged to marry her?

It was the first time he'd allowed that idea to bloom, to fully flower, in his mind. He'd thought of loving her, of making love to her, of taking her away with him, of staying in that valley with her, of showing her the whole wide world, of spending countless nights embedded in her lush, supple body. But he'd held the thought of marriage at bay, skirted it, ignored it, denied it, and now suddenly here it was in the midst of this minor catastrophe. He cursed under his breath and did it again after she told him he sounded just like Hi.

His jeans felt wet and clammy under the dark brown stain, and he wadded the Styrofoam cup into a squeaky ball, thoroughly disgusted with himself and this unending preoccupation. He thought about the nondescript motel room where he'd holed up for those four days, trying alternately to think and not to think, always coming back to this particular fantasy, that she was there with him. What if this party should cancel, too? Would she go there with him, let him lay her upon the bed...

The door opened just then, and three men pushed into the room, one of them in cowboy hat and boots.

"George!"

Laney was up and across the room in a flash, her arms outflung.

"Hey, good-lookin'!"

The tall cowboy dropped his gear and swept her up in an exuberant hug.

"Why didn't you tell us you were part of this group? We weren't expecting you!"

"I didn't know 'til just yesterd'y," he said, holding her at arm's length. "My, you're a mighty pleasant sight for sore eyes! This buddy o' mine, he was comin' up here with these other yahoos. This was his trip, and he went and got himself bashed up by a horse. Aw, he's all right. Got a busted wing, see? So I bought his place in this here posse and, well, here I am." He grinned, his reddish mustache hitching up on both ends. Laney laughed again and, catching Danzer's scowl, adroitly disengaged herself.

"George Morgan, this is Danzer Wilson, our pilot."

George turned a frank gaze on him, and Dan felt his scowl deepen. George lifted his hat in greeting.

"That's an unusual name, Danzer."

"Not so unusual," he replied tersely. "I take it you two know each other."

George Morgan grinned. "Who? Laney and me? Well, I should say we do." He slipped an arm about her shoulders and gave a squeeze. Danzer felt his blood pressure shoot up twenty points. "How long's it been, Laney girl? Couple times a year for, oh, six, seven years? Shoot, you's just a kid when I started comin' up to your place. Look at you now, all grown up and pretty as your mama."

Laney laughed. "George, you're a hoot. The folks are going to be so glad to see you."

"Lordy, it feels like going home," he said, launching into a conversation. "They okay? Kids all gone? Been any big kills this season?"

Laney answered the first two questions succinctly, but Danzer stepped in before she could relate the tale of Weir's black bear.

"Time to load up," he interjected brusquely and pushed through the small group into the hall. He was mad, damned mad, and he had no right to be. He couldn't help thinking that she hadn't bothered to mention George in her adolescent tale of boyfriends, and that fact seemed significant, ominous. What was he to think? There he was, making love to her in his mind when suddenly the door opens and she hurls herself at this tall, blond cowboy with the handlebar mustache. Nothing had gone right with this experience, not since the moment he'd set foot on her pier. What was he doing in these mountains? What had he been doing in Chicago? What was wrong with him? There was this hole in his life, this great, gaping cavity that wanted filling, and suddenly there was this woman and this wide, dangerous yearning. Somehow he had traded one black hole for another, and he was no happier, no closer to the fulfillment he'd set out to find. A cowboy! With a mustache, yet. He had to get a grip on himself.

He was in the pilot's seat, engines running, when the four of them caught up with him. George was talking a steady stream, commenting on the airplane and its various virtues. Apparently he was not only a bronc buster and an old chum but a pilot, too. Dan had heard that a lot of these Montana ranchers piloted small planes. That was understandable when the next town might be a hundred miles away, of course. Still, Hi might have said something at least—let him know about the competition.

Hi said plenty when they got back to the lodge. He said how glad he was to see George, what a grand surprise it was, how many good times they'd had. Dinner was a gab session taken up with tales about good old George and the grizzly he'd bagged that first year and the "big, rank, curly ram" whose horns had measured some fantastic length. There were tales about a moose that walked right up and knocked down the fence of the hen yard, a phantom mountain lion that they'd chased for days, the fall Hiram had taken that broke his leg and how George had hauled him home. Danzer got up and excused himself, muttering something about putting the plane to bed.

He walked out and cussed the ground for half a minute, this bad mood settling in maybe for good, then made himself go out to the plane and putter around for the sake of his conscience, if nothing else. He'd wiped and oiled and tightened just about everything he could find, and his teeth were beginning to chatter as the temperature dropped with the coming night, when he heard footsteps on the pier and looked around, hoping to see Laney, seeing George Morgan instead.

"Need any help?"

Danzer closed the engine cover and turned, wiping his hands. "Nope."

George chuckled and pushed his hat back on his head. "You don't like me much, do you?"

Dan leveled his glare. "Let's just say I wouldn't have suffered any for not having met you."

"Yeah, well, I'm not too thrilled to find you here, either. Now you know I haven't been comin' up here two, three times a year, spendin' my hard-earned money just to shoot at some big old beast."

"So?"

"So, I've had my eye on that little girl for quite some time."

"Look again," Danzer said cryptically. "That's no little girl."

"Don't think I haven't noticed," George Morgan replied. "Trouble is, she thinks of me as a kind of big brother."

Dan wasn't so sure of that, but he wasn't about to say so. He stuffed his oil rag into his rear pocket. "That's not how she thinks of me," he said bluntly.

"I guessed not," Morgan admitted. "Well, like you said, she's no little girl, and one thing about Laney, she's got a mind of her own. I s'pose she'll make it up one way or t'other. I just thought I'd be sure where you stand."

"Now you know," Dan said.

"Now we both know," George Morgan returned. He doffed his hat and turned away. Watching him go, Danzer thought he was probably a likable fellow, probably a good sort, steady, careful—and he liked him less and less. It didn't help that Hiram and Lil thought well of him, but the question was, how well did Laney like George Morgan? That he couldn't bear to truly contemplate the extent of her fondness for George was an answer itself. Now if he just knew what to do about it.

Chapter Ten

I thought you'd want to go," she argued. "I thought you came for this."

"I didn't come to watch old George bag the big one," he snapped. "Don't you ever get tired of sleeping on the ground and living out of a backpack?"

"Do you get tired of flying that plane out there?" she shot back.

"Yes."

It wasn't the answer she'd expected. It was his work, after all. And yet ... What was it about Danzer that seemed incongruous? She pushed that thought away, though once she'd seized upon it as a reason to dislike him. Dislike Danzer? She couldn't imagine anyone doing that now. Yet, George seemed to. Funny, she'd never known George to dislike anyone before, but Dan didn't seem exactly taken with George, either. Perhaps her tagging along wasn't such a good idea after all. Anyway, if Dan didn't want to go, that

was that. She didn't want to go without him. She'd just have
to tell George to break up that extra pack.

"I don't get you sometimes," she grumbled good-
naturedly, elbowing him out of the way to stack the dirty
breakfast dishes in the sink.

"I just don't want to go," he insisted, "and I don't want
you..."

She shushed him, a low noise claiming her attention. It
was a hum, a strange, far away, familiar hum. Danzer
seemed puzzled, but after a moment he heard it, too. He
straightened, the sound obviously familiar to him, too.

"That's a plane," he stated emphatically, and Laney
grabbed a towel, wiping her hands as she followed him out
the door. She tossed it over her shoulder as they rounded the
corner of the house. Hi and George were already there and
one of the men in George's party, an affable character called
Dale. Hi glanced at them and pointed to the rim of the
southern peak. Seconds later, the yellow and white plane
appeared, flying low and descending rapidly, obviously in-
tending to land.

"You guys help me," Danzer said, and the three other
men followed him in a fast trot toward the pier. The yellow
plane had landed and was taxiing through the water before
they'd managed to beach Danzer's. He left the others to
hold it and went to help their unexpected visitors secure their
craft to the end of the pier. Someone tossed him a rope, and
he tied off while a small man in a dark suit stepped cau-
tiously onto the dock.

"Dan," the man said, "good to see you. You know I
wouldn't have come if it weren't important." Laney stepped
up onto the pier, shocked to hear this man call Danzer by
name.

"Phil, dammit, you weren't supposed to come at all. The
board gave me a year, Phillip, not a few lousy weeks."

"It's all coming apart, Dan," the man argued. "The whole Mexican plant deal. Washington's yelling about the Arab faction, and Japan's getting cold feet."

"It's a done deal, Phillip. You know that. Let Washington yell all it wants. We've got all the *t*'s crossed and all the *i*'s dotted. They can't stop that deal. Japan knows that. The Arabs know that. *You* know that!"

"But it needs a strong hand, Dan, someone to see it through."

"Let Wallace Clark see it through. We chose him just for that purpose!"

"Dan, I can't believe this is you. I thought you'd be tired of this foolish game by now. I'm tired of it, I can tell you that, and so is the rest of the board. You're an adult, Dan, and no grown-up takes off to play three months at a time! We need you back in Chicago. You have a business to run there and obligations to meet. You have a real life there, Dan. When are you going to stop playing these silly games and face up to that?"

"I'm not sure I am!" Danzer shot back. "And who the hell are you to tell me where my life is and isn't, what my obligations are? I have an obligation to myself, you know, and if I want to fulfill that by spending three months in the mountains and three months at sea or three months on the moon, it's none of your business!"

The man named Phillip shook his head sorrowfully. "I'm sorry you feel that way, Dan, because everything you've accomplished is about to pass out of your hands to someone else. The board wants you back but, failing that, has instructed me to offer you your walking papers."

Laney could tell that Dan was more affected by this than he wanted to show. Her head was reeling with what she'd heard. The board, a Mexican deal, Washington, Japan, *Arabs*? What did it all mean? She looked at her father, saw he was as confused as she, and switched her gaze back to

Danzer. She realized again how little she knew about this man. Where was he going when he left here? Would he be back? Had he ever intended to sustain this relationship? He wanted her, but did he love her? He hadn't said so. He hadn't said much of anything, certainly not about himself. Suddenly she felt like a horrible fool.

"I tried to resign months ago," Danzer was saying. "I don't need the job, and I don't want the job. So don't try this bullying act on me. You've wasted your time, Phillip."

"And you aren't wasting yours, Dan? Good grief, man, you had a great job with a lifetime guarantee! How can you just throw that away?"

"Easy," Danzer said. "Easiest thing I've ever done."

Phillip shook his head. "Well, you're a rich man. I suppose you can do as you wish. I just hate to see you wasting your talents like this. You know what your problem is, don't you? You just don't know what you want. You never have. Maybe you never will."

"I know what I *don't* want, Phil," Danzer said. "I don't want to be hamstrung, stifled. I don't want to be shackled. I don't want to be always fulfilling someone else's expectations of me." Laney closed her eyes, each word a blow.

"I've heard this speech before," Phillip objected in a resigned voice. "I didn't understand it then, and I still don't, but I guess I understand this: you're not coming back to the firm, are you, Dan?"

"It's just not for me, Phil," Danzer told him.

"I had to give it a shot," the other man said, and he offered his hand. Dan took it willingly.

"Give my regards to the board. I'll be in touch."

"You were the best in the business, old man."

"Maybe I will be again some day, Phil, but on my terms, no one else's."

The two men took their leave of each other, surprisingly more friendly than when they'd begun the conversation.

Laney watched them, smarting from the things she'd heard. So he didn't want to be shackled. He didn't want to be responsible to anyone else. No wonder he was scared of this involvement. No wonder he couldn't just let himself love her. This was all a big game to him, a fantasy, a bit of play-acting. And in her heart she had thought it would be forever. Apparently nothing was forever with Danzer Wilson. She bit her lip, thinking of those moments when he could have taken so much more than he had. She supposed she should thank him for that much, but somehow she just couldn't be grateful. She wasn't sure she could even be civil at the moment.

As the yellow plane revved its engines and pulled away from the dock, George stepped to Laney's side. It was like him, she thought absently, to notice her distress. Danzer stood where he was for several moments, his hand lifted to shade his eyes as the small craft turned, picked up speed and lifted off. Danzer gave a wave and turned away, his gaze taking in the whole group, Hiram and Dale on the ropes of the partly beached plane, and Laney, with George standing at her elbow. Only Dale seemed inclined to look away, pretending he hadn't overheard.

Danzer ducked his head a bit. "Sorry about that," he said.

"I'll bet you are," Laney spoke up. "I'll bet you're real sorry to have your little game interrupted before you've even actually scored!"

Danzer's mouth fell open. "What are you talking about?"

"I heard him," she said, throwing up an arm to point at the southern horizon. "We all heard him, Dan. This is a game to you. No wonder you wouldn't...couldn't..." She dared not say it, not in front of her father and her friend and a total stranger. She didn't want them to know what a Class A idiot she was, that it was only his fear of involvement, his

detachment that had prevented her from making a com
plete fool of herself. He had never intended to stay, neve
intended to take her away with him; probably he had neve
even considered either option. Suddenly she couldn't bea
it any longer. She covered her face with both hands, burs
into tears and turned blindly away. It was George wh
caught her, reaching out with both arms to comfort her
Sweet George. He was more like a brother than anyone sh
had ever known.

"There now, honey," George crooned, but it was Dan
zer's approaching footsteps that she heard.

"Laney," he said in a surprisingly normal voice.

"I think she's heard about all she needs to," George pu
in, his arms wrapped protectively around her.

"And I think you ought to butt out," Danzer state
threateningly. "This is between Laney and me."

"There's nothing between us!" she declared, whirlin
suddenly. "It was all a game! Why don't you just admit it?"

"You don't understand," he insisted. "It's not wha
you've made it out to be."

"Don't you think I know that now?" she cried.

"Laney, dammit, listen to me!" he ordered, and sud
denly everyone was shouting. George yelled at Danzer, an
Danzer yelled at George, and Dale then screamed the plan
was floating away, while Hiram shouted for everyone t
calm down. Laney bolted, their voices echoing inside he
head, tears streaming from her eyes, one hateful though
making everything else irrelevant. It wasn't love. It wasn'
love. Whatever it was, it obviously wasn't love.

There was only one place to go, but she doubted even h
would truly understand. The tears made the trees and rock
swim before her eyes, but she knew the way instinctively
She had walked it in the dark on a moonless night, in a
driving rain and the blinding snow. She thought of all Crater
had told her, and it seemed like so much nonsense now, de

signed to cater to her own selfish, silly desires. Crater would do that for her, and he knew at times what she was feeling even before she did. It all made awful, perfect sense.

She ran most of the way, oblivious to the chill despite the fact that she'd worn no jacket and the temperature subtly dropped as she climbed higher. At the end she was almost crawling in her scramble to get over the rocky ledges and outcroppings, skinning her palms and knees like the reckless adolescent she once was. She met him coming down the mountain, his white hair flying on the wind, his blanket poncho flapping around his leather leggings. She burst into tears at the sight of him, felt herself lifted to her feet, the rough, heavily pilled wool on her cheek, his thin, ropy arm about her shoulders.

He didn't ask, and she didn't tell him. She didn't have to. He knew well enough what it would take to break her heart. Back in the cave she sobbed a bit upon his cot, then sat stoically by the fire and let the tears roll silently down her cheeks. Finally she dried up, numb to all but a small voice in the back of her head that repeated maliciously the same refrain. "It was just a game, little fool, just a game."

Crater made a pot of coffee and went out, leaving it steaming in the edge of the coals. She barely noticed. The toasty aroma filled her nostrils but failed to register in her brain. The sound of his movements reached her ears and left no impression, triggered no thought. His person passed from her view, yet she did not notice. She had closed in on herself, shut down, turned off everything but that small, ugly voice.

"Let go of me!" Danzer snatched his arm from George's grip. George braced his feet and cocked his fist. *Southpaw*, thought Danzer, and lifted his left hand, too late. George's knuckles connected sharply with his cheekbone, rocking him backward and into the grass. Everything rotated a half turn

and back again. Danzer expected anger, hot and strong, but
it didn't come. He felt only resignation and distaste. It was
what he deserved, after all. He should have told her, should
have accepted with joy and grace what he had found here.
He was a coward who bemoaned the lack of that which he
could not bring himself to take. It had been within his grasp
all along, and he had done nothing more than touch and tell
himself it probably wasn't good for him. He pushed himself up from the ground and faced George.

"That one's free," he said. "The next one's going to cost
you."

George glared at him. "Name your price," and he wound
up that hard left.

Danzer blocked it and then the right. He stepped into the
third, and it whizzed by his shoulder. He flattened both
hands on George's solid chest and shoved. The cowboy went
down, boots kicking up tails of dust. Danzer looked down
on him.

"We can beat each other senseless but that won't change
anything," he stated quickly. George got his feet under him
and stood.

"You had to play with her, didn't you?" George chal-
lenged, fists coming up. Dan began to circle warily.

"It wasn't like that. That's what I tried *not* to do."

"You did a poor job then."

"Agreed, but this won't solve anything."

"It might."

"It won't change the fact that she loves me, George."

The cowboy stopped, eyes narrowing, fists aloft. He
didn't like that, wouldn't easily accept it. His lean face
hardened with resolve, and Dan steeled himself, his hand
folding into weapons. He'd fight every way he could. This
was one he wasn't going to lose, for all their sakes.

George stepped up, and Dan sighted his solar plexus, in-
tending to get him down with one hard blow that would

rive the wind out of him. It was coming, that next rocking
unch, more serious than anything that had yet been
hrown. It was coming. He could feel it on his chin and
owered his head, prepared, determined.

Hiram stepped between them. "He's right, George, dead
ight."

That settled it, tamped it down. Dan felt a great strength
ardening within him, a certainty he hadn't known for a
ong time. It was like coming out of a hole into the light, like
waking from a long, deep, dream-filled sleep. George's fists
wavered and slowly sank, the resolve drained from his face.
He glared at Dan.

"What're you going to do about her?" he demanded.

Dan straightened and opened his hands. "I'm going to
narry her," he said. "If I can find her."

He turned and started off in the direction she had fled.

"Dan?"

He halted at the sound of her father's voice. "What?" He
lidn't make it friendly, didn't make it patient.

"What that man said, I just want to know about how you
tand."

He faced him. "I don't get it."

Hiram spread his work-roughened hands. "He said
ou're a rich man, a big man."

"So?"

"There's got to be a purpose in life, a reason to go on
eing a man, rich or otherwise."

Danzer widened his stance, shoulders square, chin level.

"I'm not going to spend the rest of my life sitting on my
ackside, if that's what you're getting at. I need to build a
ife for myself same as any man. I think I know how to be-
;in now."

Hiram held his gaze a long moment, testing, weighing.
Finally he nodded.

"You want help lookin'?"

"No." It was expected, accepted.

"You've learned something then, but be careful. She's most likely gone to Crater, and that old man's not as reasonable as I am. He don't have to be."

Danzer thought on that. Maybe it was supposed to come to this. What Hi had said was true. A man had to have a reason to go on being a man, and he'd found his. He looked at George, thought of Crater. Maybe he had to prove what he was willing to do for her. It just seemed right. He turned away, knowing finally how it had to be, what he wanted. The last thing he saw was Dale wading waist-deep into the lake after his plane. He didn't turn back. He didn't even think of it.

How many hours she sat there by the fire, Laney neither knew nor cared. Crater came in and cooked up some camp biscuits for lunch. He dipped them in the strong, rank coffee he'd made up earlier. The flour tasted moldy and old and the coffee was bitter, but Crater was used to it, and Laney didn't eat. She cleaned up after him, though, welcoming the familiar task. She carried the bowl and the pan and the fork he'd used to the back of the cavern where the ceiling hung low and a trickle of water gathered in a natural rock basin. Crouching, she scrubbed them with sand and rinsed them out, then carried them back to the rough, open shelf which comprised his kitchen.

She looked around her, needing something, anything, to do. Mechanically she moved to the hard cot and started to straighten the covers, but soon a deep lethargy crept over her, and she lay down instead. The planks were hard and rough beneath the blankets and skins, and she had the fleeting thought that long ago this had been the norm. She wondered, for the first time, why he did it, why Crater lived this way. She knew suddenly that this was not for her. She wanted to understand it, wanted to experience it and to

now she could come back to it, but she didn't want to
pend her years in a bygone century, a past life, an era dead
o all but dreams and visions. She wished she had known
nis before, was thankful she knew it now. Could she find a
ob in Seattle? She closed her eyes and concentrated on that,
rying to conjure a face that eluded her now, fleeing deeper
nd deeper into the shadows of her mind until she followed
into sleep.

A long time later, Laney jerked awake, her mind search-
ng recent memory for the noise that had startled her. It
ame again, roaring, cracking, overtaking its own echo, and
he bolted upright, eyes wide. A gunshot, a long bore rifle,
Crater's old piece. She tore across the sand, careered into the
assage, bounced off the thick rock walls. He never hunted
o close to the cave, seldom used the old rifle for anything
xcept scaring off curious critters that wanted to make a
laim to his natural haven. Somehow she knew that wasn't
he case this time.

The passage narrowed enough to make running difficult.
he slowed to a fast walk, sliding along one wall, until it
idened again, and then she was there. Crater was hun-
ered down behind the twin pines, his rifle muzzle propped
n a rock jammed into the narrow space between them. Well
eyond, belly down on the ground, Danzer Wilson peered
ut from behind a boulder. Every nerve in Laney's body
uddenly tensed. When Crater thumbed back the hammer,
he click sent her jumping. She grabbed the barrel and
anked it up, the discharge nearly wrenching it from her
and and propelling Crater backward onto his rear end. A
ree branch came crashing down in a shower of needles and
wigs. She flung the gun as far from her as she could.

"You know better than to take potshots at people!"

Crater scrambled up, his eyes wild. "I wasn't aimin' at
im! I hit what I shoot at!"

So he did. Laney glared at him and twisted away, throwing herself into the notch in the rock.

"He'll be comin'!" the old man called after her. "He's on his way! You ready for that?"

"No!" she screamed, skinning her elbows on both walls as the passage narrowed. She wasn't ready for that, but she wasn't ready to see him wounded—or worse—either. Still, the thought of having to face him, of hearing the apologies and the justifications, was nauseatingly distasteful, but what was she to do? The indecision stopped her.

Crater shouted at Danzer to stay put, and Danzer shouted that he was coming up. Laney cringed. She felt trapped, cornered. She turned back, the walls seeming to close in on her. They were arguing, the two men, one saying to step aside, the other suggesting a warmer destination for his opponent. She stumbled onto the scene without really knowing what she was doing. Danzer stood just below Crater in the clear space before the pines, feet planted, arms flexed.

"I don't want to knock you down, old man," he was saying, "but I will."

"It won't do you any good," she said, already regretting the impulse to speak. Danzer's head came up as she stepped from behind the trees, the dark eyes sharp and direct. There was a bruise on his cheek and a tiny cut high up on the bone. She looked away, her insides twisted with conflicting emotions. Crater spoke to her over his shoulder.

"Go on inside, child. He ain't comin' in."

"Don't think you're going to stop me," Danzer warned. "It's taken me hours to track her this far—" He paused and she found herself glancing at him. His eyes waited, pointed, determined. Hers skittered away. "I won't be stopped now," he told them both.

"Go away, Dan," she pleaded. "I don't want your explanations. I don't want you."

"Well, I want you," he said, starting forward. Crater
ocked his way, stepping to one side with surprising agil-
y. Anger flashed across Danzer's face, and he steadied
mself with a calming breath. "The last man that tried to
op me hit the dirt," he informed him.

"That's not all he hit by the looks of your face," Crater
ckled.

"I'm here, aren't I?" Dan pointed out. "I'm here, and
m tired, and I'm running out of patience fast! Now get out
my way."

The old man studied his opponent, the stubborn set of his
w, the taut line of his mouth, the flash of his eye, the fur-
w of his brow. Slowly his arms relaxed at his sides, and he
rned to Laney, craning his head at the end of his long, thin
ck as if to say, "It's up to you now." He grunted and sat
ght down, arms draped over his bony knees.

Laney couldn't believe her eyes. When had Crater ever
andoned her? When had he failed to know that she
eded his protection? She blinked at the sight of him
uatting there on the ground, taking himself out of it.

Danzer moved toward her, and she reacted like a wild
imal, bolting instinctively. She knew it was foolish, and
e hadn't gone five steps before his hand closed on the back
her shirt, the fabric drew taut, and she was hauled up
ort. She yanked herself free, but his hands were at her
ms, grasping, trapping. Frustrated, she lashed out, her
and slapping air. Suddenly he was thrusting her away.

"All right, hit me! If it'll make you feel better, hit me!
eorge did. Crater tried to. Maybe I even deserve it!"

Laney's brows puckered with the impulse to touch the
ruise on his cheek. Crater hadn't done that.

"George hit you?" she said. "Why did George hit you?"

Dan gave her an exasperated look. "Because he's in love
ith you, Laney. Didn't you know that?"

George in love with her? How could he be in love with her? She didn't feel that way about him, but then that didn't matter, did it? Why had she thought love was always a mutual thing? She suddenly felt such sorrow for poor George George who was like a brother to her. She looked at Danzer with brimming eyes.

"Did you hurt him?" she asked.

"No," he answered bitterly, then gently, "Well, yes suppose I did, but not with my fists. With words. I told him I was going to marry you."

Laney reeled backward, jaw dropping, arm flying "What? I-I don't understand."

"Don't you?" Danzer asked softly. "Then maybe I' better explain it again." His hand slid down her arm, rai ing gooseflesh all over her body through her sleeve, and the she felt herself gathered into his arms. His head bowed to ward hers, his mouth drawing slowly closer. She told her self not to let this happen and knew she couldn't stop i Nothing had changed as far as her body was concerned, an nothing was going to. His mouth settled over hers, tender at first, then with growing demands. She kept her arms her sides, but there was no denying the response of her body

It was as if every nerve clamored to be touched, sated, if each one took on a life and a will of its own. She did n mean to let her eyes close, to melt against him. She did n intend to allow him to fit her body so blatantly to his, to pa her mouth and plumb its depths. She did not want to fe that fire licking up through her belly, to tremble where h hands caressed, pressed, skimmed. She did not want to wa him, to need him so. But she did, and slowly it dawned c her that this was how it must have been with him. He hadn intended to hurt her, hadn't wanted to get in too deep a yet..."

Somehow she found the strength to push away, to bre that erotic spell his touch always produced. It was then th

Crater chortled and got up and went inside. Laney shot a narrowed look at him but spared him no thought.

"Who was that man?" she demanded, keeping her distance. He folded his arms as if to assure her that he would not touch her again without her permission.

"First vice president of one of the largest banking institutions in the country."

She wasn't surprised. "You worked for him?"

"He worked for me."

That was unexpected. "Then you were..."

"Unhappy," he said.

"You gave up that high-powered job," she said, "to come here and work for next to nothing."

"I gave up that high-powered job for a chance at happiness," he told her. "It was pure luck that brought me here first. It just worked out that way. You can't understand, Laney, because you've never been dissatisfied in the way I was. You've never wondered if your life was over before it had begun. You've never yearned for something you couldn't even identify."

"Haven't I?" she answered quietly. "I think I have, but because I couldn't identify it, I denied it. Maybe I did that because I couldn't face the change that would come with having what I wanted."

"We're not so different then, are we?" he said softly, and she felt a smile beginning.

"I guess not."

"You didn't want to fall in love with me," he pointed out, and she lifted her chin, her gaze steady.

"No, I didn't."

"I didn't want to fall in love with you, either, at least not the way I have."

The tears and the laughter began at the same time. "Wh-when did you know?"

"When *George* showed up," he admitted sheepishly. "Until then I tried to believe it was purely physical."

She wiped at the tears, a smile firmly in place. "If it was purely physical, why didn't you . . ."

"Make love to you?" he asked huskily, and she nodded, her eyes never leaving his. "Because I knew what it meant to you. I guess I just couldn't take advantage of that. It seemed cheap and unfair, and maybe that's what love is all about, wanting to protect the other person more than you want to please yourself."

"I—I love you," she whispered, trying not to cry.

"I know," he said and opened his arms. She fell into them, hanging her own about his neck. "I love you, too."

They held each other tightly for a long, precious moment, then Laney let her head fall back, her hair covering his arm.

"Poor George," she said, and Danzer wrapped his hand in her hair.

"Poor George nearly broke my face." She went up on tiptoe and straightened to gently kiss the mark on his cheek, his hand dragging in her hair. "Poor George," he whispered, his arm tightening about her waist. "Oh, I love you!"

"Hey!"

Crater's shout stopped the slow descent of her lips to his. Danzer grimaced and released her to turn toward the voice. Laney laughed. The old man was holding a battered cardboard box from which the words and pictures had long ago been worn. Crater held it out.

"You play chess?"

Danzer looked at Laney. She lifted her arm and hooked her hand over his shoulder.

"Well," she said, "if you're going to marry me, you have to like a challenge." Danzer smiled.

"I'll beat your socks off, old man."

"Ain't wearing any!" Crater cackled and disappeared inside the notch, motioning for them to follow. They started off together, arm in arm. Then Danzer suddenly stopped.

"Wait a minute," he said. "We may have a problem."

She sobered instantly. "What?"

"We know you don't get airsick, but do you get seasick?"

"Of course not! I've spent half my life on that river down there. Why?"

"Well, because," he teased, "you're going to spend your honeymoon at sea, six months of it, anyway. You'll like Africa, though. I'm sure of that."

"*Africa!*" Laney gasped. "You don't mean it!"

"Oh, it's all arranged. There's that sloop going to New Guinea, then the safari—it won't be as rough as what you're used to—and three months in the Caribbean. Hm, guess I'll have to forget that Honduran beauty, as long as you're willing to give up poor George, that is."

She leaned against him, her temple pressed to his cheek. "There isn't a man in this world I could love like I love you," she whispered, and he locked his arms around her.

"I can't wait to let you demonstrate that! But first..." He unlocked his arms and held them up. "Unhand me, woman, I have to prove I'm worthy of you." She stepped back, hands on hips.

"Combat on the field of chess," she said, adding, "Better let him win!"

He gave her a shocked face and grabbed her hand, then smiled. "I intend to!" he said, pulling her toward the notch.

She laughed, and then they slipped inside, her hand in his, the sound echoing down into the valley.

* * * * *

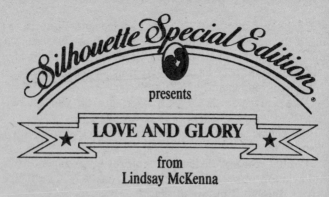

Silhouette Special Edition

presents

★ LOVE AND GLORY ★

from
Lindsay McKenna

Introducing a gripping new series celebrating our men—and women—in uniform. Meet the Trayherns, a military family as proud and colorful as the American flag, a family fighting the shadow of dishonor, a family determined to triumph—with LOVE AND GLORY!

June: **A QUESTION OF HONOR** (SE #529) leads the fast-paced excitement. When Coast Guard officer Noah Trayhern offers Kit Anderson a safe house, he unwittingly endangers his own guarded emotions.

July: **NO SURRENDER** (SE #535) Navy pilot Alyssa Trayhern's assignment with arrogant jet jockey Clay Cantrell threatens her career—and her heart—with a crash landing!

August: **RETURN OF A HERO** (SE #541) Strike up the band to welcome home a man whose top-secret reappearance will make headline news . . . with a delicate, daring woman by his side.

Silhouette Intimate Moments

NOW APPEARING!

LIEUTENANT
GABRIEL RODRIGUEZ
in
Something of Heaven

From his first appearance in Marilyn Pappano's popular *Guilt by Association*, Lieutenant Gabriel Rodriguez captured readers' hearts. Your letters poured in, asking to see this dynamic man reappear—this time as the hero of his own book. This month, all your wishes come true in *Something of Heaven* (IM #294), Marilyn Pappano's latest romantic tour de force.

Gabriel longs to win back the love of Rachel Martinez, who once filled his arms and brought beauty to his lonely nights. Then he drove her away, unable to face the power of his feelings and the cruelty of fate. That same fate has given him a second chance with Rachel, but to take advantage of it, he will have to trust her with his darkest secret: somewhere in the world, Gabriel may have a son. Long before he knew Rachel, there was another woman, a woman who repaid his love with lies—and ran away to bear their child alone. Rachel is the only one who can find that child for him, but if he asks her, will he lose her love forever or, together, will they find *Something of Heaven*?

This month only, read *Something of Heaven* and follow Gabriel on the road to happiness.

You'll flip . . . your pages won't!
Read paperbacks *hands-free* with

Book Mate • I

The perfect "mate" for all your romance paperbacks
Traveling • Vacationing • At Work • In Bed • Studying
• Cooking • Eating

Perfect size for all standard paperbacks, this wonderful invention makes reading a pure pleasure! Ingenious design holds paperback books OPEN and FLAT so even wind can't ruffle pages — leaves your hands free to do other things. Reinforced, wipe-clean vinyl-covered holder flexes to let you turn pages without undoing the strap . . . supports paperbacks so well, they have the strength of hardcovers!

Pages turn WITHOUT opening the strap

SEE-THROUGH STRAP

Reinforced back stays flat

Built in bookmark

BOOK MARK

BACK COVER HOLDING STRIP

10 x 7¼ opened
Snaps closed for easy carrying, too

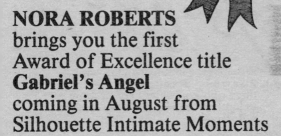

17 41 278 38 35